THE BONE JAR

SHEAL MULLIN-BERUBE
LARISA HUNTER

ISBN13: 978-1-959350-28-6

Set in: Marion 12pt, Catalina Typewriter 12pt, Resquro Halloween Font 24/48pt

USA/CANADA

All serial killers want to win. They choose victims they can kill successfully. -Pat Brown

❧

"In writing, you must kill all your darlings."-William Faulkner

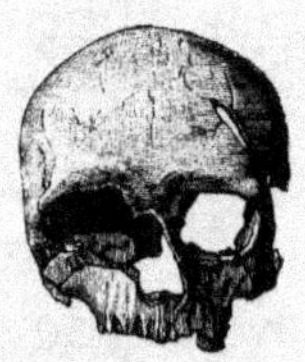

THE SINNER BEARING THE WITNESS

All towns have their secrets. Some buried in the ground, others buried in the quiet dark places of the home in which no one dares enter. In this town three would be bound in events that would lead them to the place in which we end this tale, a place covered in blood and spit and sex, all twisted and rotten and laid bear. It is a tale in which we know and learn of the secrets kept within those dark places. There are times in which the secrets stay buried and there are times when they rise to the surface. It seems impossible that they remain forever lost to time, but there are people in this world who never know what darkness lurked in the heart of those they loved and hated.

Houses themselves hold in them the wounds of the screams, the pain, the sorrow, the truth, they remain forever a place in which we find that the darkened rooms are darkened for a reason and they are a prison for some. The unlikely twist of fate is not that unlikely if you think about it. All small towns have them. The threads that bind us are tight, tighter than we care to admit. It's not unlikely that you sitting there reading this could have been a kid, like us, stuck in a small town, surrounded by weirdos, losers, rejects, the kids that are always the ones seen as delinquents. We were the ones that the town labeled and marked and put bounty on. In this town, we buried our secrets, but, as it turns out, they were not buried that deep.

In reflection, we should have burnt them, and buried the ashes so that none could remember or recall what happened in that shit hole town. Instead the dead did not stay buried, instead the dead revealed what secrets they held, instead three friends went out into the world cemented with a memory that would haunt them, and yet they don't remember it, at least for now, they don't know the secret yet and neither do you. It was found in the pages of the dairies that set themselves on the desk of the FBI, it was scrolled out in rushed strokes of pens that were held by those who would find themselves wound and bound in murder.

When the pages were then placed out for the public to see, would they see people who were actually human? Would they understand that no one begins evil? That evil sometimes is marked on a person like a deep penetrating scar. Some of us are able to rise up above the things that lurked in our rooms, and some of us are not, it's never certain what makes you the thing you are. In retrospect, if things went differently, there would be, I suspect a little house somewhere and in that house would be two lovers sprawling out in front of a warm fire, playing with the children they had bore. There would be an Ivy bringing her lover another piece of pie, a Troy bouncing little Charles on his lap. The others who placed themselves in the path of this story would be wherever it is that people end up, all living lives of no real consequence, but living nonetheless.

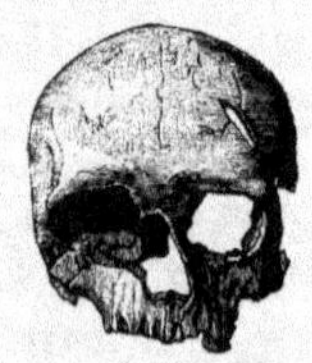

FROM THE DIARY OF IVY

In retrospect, it seems unlikely that one can just erase oneself, but, it's surprisingly easy to find people that know how to do that. There is a box, to which the location of, is not something I wish to explain or tell you, in which lies the names of those that I took, stole, altered, destroyed. I killed them in a way. Each one, I took, changing my name, again and again.

Disappearing myself with hair dye and cut this way and that. Contacts to change my eyes, outfits that could be 'normal'. I blended myself into the 'normals'. If you don't believe me, how many times have you seen Jane Doe? Do you know that this woman is who she says she is? Do you know if this young boy who may not be physically so, is what he claims to be? Just like a bandage on a wounded doll, I could bind my breasts and take names like Tom and George.

I could alter my hair and be Cherry or Tiny. The harder part was to claim a space to sleep, a space to eat. The nameless and invisible are unlikely to gain trust. The 'street kids' are the ones you ignore, that you spit words like 'bum' at, the ones that may find themselves in the lap of a man driving a Prius, just for a tin of food. We were desperate and clawing, just like animals reaching for help. Like the dolls in my room, there was nothing but dead eyes looking back at us. Dead eyes that held no help, no hope, no food, no shelter, and so it was only cold, only emptiness that cradled me. In the windswept streets I lumbered and lingered, like a shaded shadow, like a ghost, and yet none helped me.

None held me, but then again, what did I expect, my father always told me, "Out there you will get nothing, out there they will try and kill you"

OK "dad". That one I will give you. Out here there are monsters just like you.

It was always this wasn't it. This caused my blood to flow into the pit in which I lay. How was it that this was your fate. The memories of it seem so blurry, and yet here I sit, muddling it over. It seems that you would suspect that this girl whom you lay bare in this manner, cold and slabbed in the chilly room in which the slumber and silence of others fill with an inaudible sigh that twists darkly in the heart of those who witness it.

It is a reminder of the broken doll they had when they were young, the putrid suffering that is life, it is the dark and the dirt and it's there, naked and unafraid of your judgment. I don't know how I became this, but as I sit here playing with the slimy bits of what was once a human no doubt, now ripped and raw in my hands like ground beef, my thoughts turned to the past. It is in the moments when we are lost and afraid that the past floods in like shards of glass.

It cuts us deep, filling us with pain, sometimes reflecting moments of joy, but more when you are a damaged doll like me, they are only pain. Pain is something we know well. I have met in my time, others like me. It is not that uncommon that a poor little girl becomes slave to the rhythms of abuse. I am not the first to have their bodies given over like goods at a market. There are hundreds of us, thousands, maybe millions.

Boys too, let's not forget them, there are many boys who have felt what I have felt, who have seared into their flesh the marks of the past. You know them, even if they hide behind many layers, even if they are afraid to show you that scar or this wound, they are there, sitting there right now no doubt. To deny this fact, is to deny truth.

Many of you do. You would like to blame what I was wearing no doubt, tell me I deserved it. Whatever, I am not living anymore to be affected by their stings, your words of judgment matter not to those who are here with me. This place, the 'after' is not a lonely place, nor is it a place of torment.

It is a place for those who were unloved, for those you condemned, it is for those who were good, and evil, there is no judgment here, only darkness. My world began in the same way as everyone else, I was born in no great way, it was typical by all accounts. I was born with little probably of being 'normal.' My mother had lost a child already, and died in her crib.

My birth signaled for her a triggered and deep thought that lingered there in her heart, and so instead of a hidden kiss that was laced into the face of the mother in Wendy's Peter Pan, my mother's mouth held back a whimper. I was a reminder of both joy and suffering, and she held me at arm's length, wanting to love, yet fearing to love. I recall now the times in my youth, in which my silence was paid for by the gifts of fluffy white bears that flooded in my room, surrounding me with their empty eyes, one for every beating.

The spiraling dead eyed teddy bears suffocating me with the memory of whatever it was that brought them into my world. There were dolls too, and yes he paid for each sin, with gifts of little necklaces, emblazoned and engraved with sick words like Daddy's Girl. Each of the things I kept around me, was like a scar. I sat on my bed, holding another one, this one named Darla was a funny little rag doll with red hair. I squeezed her neck, as if killing the memory of the thing over and over, I hated this doll.

I recall the days in which the world was simpler, when it was all just skipping on the black top over numbers haphazardly sketched in cheap white chalk. It was on a cool fall day where I met two of the most dearest friends, that I fear, are also two that I regret involving in the making of me. This making, was their unmaking, and I was the thing that corrupted them, I was that rising darkness that creeps into the room as light is slowly dissolved by the moonlight until it snuffs out the light at last. I was sitting by the swings one morning, grabbing clumps of dirt.

I was not a kid that enjoyed recess, I viewed school as a place that at least for a while would be one free of abuse, and where I could just retreat into my own little 'wonderland' full of bugs and blood and gore and yes, I was the 'weird kid'. In fact the kid that made other mothers warn you of.

I am the 'thing' they say, that would be the monster in this case, but I was just a little girl, a little broken doll that was marked and stained and destroyed. I was Darla with the hands strangling, suffocating, starving, shutting out the light. I hate that doll, she is all that I am, and it kills me. I looked up in time to see the 'Dumpster Kid' run by. What was that one's name again? Couldn't remember. That one lived in foster care down the street, a weird one. Quiet, like me.

The other one up the street ran by after, I suspected he was chasing Dumpster Kid again. Troy was that one's name, he could be mean sometimes but nice too. He lived with his aunt from what I'd heard because his mother had died and his daddy had left a long time before that. Him and the Dumpster Kid played chase a lot in the school yard but I'd also seen Troy beat on the other kid and tease the Dumpster Kid a few times. Seemed they had a hate but love relationship. Dumpster Kid, now wasn't that a nickname. Kids can be cruel can't they, it was a term we all used for the forgotten, orphaned kids, the ones that didn't have parents or family. Troy at least had his aunt, Dumpster Kid didn't even have that.

"HEY!"

It startled me, making me turn around and look back over my shoulder. There stood Troy staring at me with this weird smirk on his face and Dumpster Kid's head in a headlock. Dumpster Kid was struggling to get out from under Troy's grip, it only made Troy clamp down harder and start laughing at the kid. A muffled whimper and I was up off the ground to take a swing at Troy for being mean. I guess he saw it coming and let the Dumpster Kid go at the last second to catch my fist and look me straight in the eye.

"What's that for huh?"

"You aren't being very nice you know," I grunted back at him, yanking my fist out of his hand, "leave the kid be, you're supposed to be a friend."

"I'm okay." Came the soft voice from below us, making both of us look down and stare at the kid sitting on the ground at our feet.

Troy and I looked back at each other and cracked up into a fit of giggles. The Dumpster Kid joined in cautiously at first then started guffawing like crazy. Turned out, the three of us would become very close over that summer. Closer than most people would ever become. Like our own little band of misfits on our own little island just for us. Staring off in the distance, I felt myself perhaps, safe for a moment, safe with these rejected misfits, perhaps even she could finally find peace. My mind wandered around its dark corners, but there were 'things' I was not ready to share with them yet. They were wandering down to the river, it was hot that day and with the recess bell came the end of school and freedom.

"First one in the lake, has to kiss a slimy snake" yelled Dumpster Kid, Ivy pulled back at Troy's shirt to ensure that she would be the first to splash in.

"You guys are so stupid" she yelled back

Troy and Dumpster Kid leapt in after me, and that is when Troy seemed to notice something about me that he didn't notice before. I didn't like that at all, he was staring and it made me nervous.

"Hey, what's that bruise on your arm?" Troy said, pulling my arm forward to reveal a series of finger shaped bruises.

"Nothing", I replied, trying to hide my wrist under the water

Troy dropped it but I felt he knew. It was something in his eyes. Kids who live with monsters know each other, as if they all are living in the same fog filled land which is only visible to them, and each of them are marked with arrows over their head only visible by fellow kids of monsters.

It was a look of pity, mixed with anger. The summer scrolled on, and life was good for a while. They spent time at the Bowl-a-Rama and down at the cheesy penny arcade. Troy and Dumpster would come by her house on their bikes, and off they went, free from cares, free from the monsters, running, always running, and hiding, but they were free. The next time they saw the truth, was in an unfortunate meeting with me when I was sitting outside my house holding a silly red-haired doll. I had my head down.

"Hey, want to go down to the corner store for slushies?" Asked Dumpster Kid

"Not today", I replied through tears

Troy got off his Radio-Flyer bike, and jumped up the stairs to sit with me, he reached towards my face, pulled back my hair, and there it was. My eye was black and sullen, and swollen.

"You too huh?", Troy asked, "Auntie does it to me too at my house" he continued, lifting up his sleeve to reveal the cigarette burns marking up his skin

I looked into Troy's eyes with deep pain, and leaned my head into his lap, and wept. Troy sat there stroking my hair, just humming at me oddly, while Dumpster sat one step below me and held my knee.

"They are all assholes," said Dumpster, "parents..." he continued almost spitting the word, "they don't care about you, once they push you out your just trash, garbage, it's fucking stupid"

I wiped the tears from my eyes, and we all gathered up our bikes.

"Come on, lets get out of here, show them they can't break us, show them we are not their fucking property" Troy said

Off we went, down the lane and that was the beginning of it, the beginning of the knowing of the horrors we would face, all of us knew what it was that bound us, the threads of abuse, wound like hands strangling the neck of the little doll, but this was not the only fact that fused us. That was still a thing yet to be discovered, yet to be revealed. The summer went on fairly unadventurous, with us three friends cementing the bonds stronger.

ଓ

Kisses were stolen by Troy and given by Ivy, Dumpster Kid even had a few flirtations, all of them sharing laughter and love as the fireflies kept watch. It is in the floating of time, that we are lost now, moving forward and backward in the story we tell. Stories are like that, they often begin somewhere and end somewhere. The town in which these misfits, these souls find themselves sitting there holding the secrets that they tried to bury but they have surfaced and there by a tree in a place known only to them, there is a doll in a box and there is dirt, and blood.

Time is a funny thing, and sometimes time can be overlooked and forgotten. The past can be left behind on a road somewhere, where the cross roads blur into the highways and byways, leading out of our shit hole town. It was at these crossroads that the hands bound together in dirt, in blood, in dolls were broken, unclasped and left behind. In the pages of the diaries that lay on the desk of the FBI, were pieces of lives, not the entire moment, and when the stories are retold, they are often quoted by those who bore witness.

We may not know the entire story of the three of them, we may not understand what these small snapshots frozen in time would ever reveal as to the 'why' of it all. But the fact is, that sometimes there are things that bind stronger than friendship, stronger than love, than family, and these iron bindings are often forged through something far more sinister.

It is the chains of the things that have been witnessed, the horror burned in the eyes of a child, the marks on the bodies of those that bore them, they are the chains of blood, of death, of knifes and secrets, and those secrets, the ones that hide in the darkened rooms, in the closed shutters of 'that house' on your street. The chains that wind and bind through our hearts, and yet these chains can be hidden, even by our own mind, and we forget that we had them. We forget who we knew, what we did and in the mind we build metal boxes fused around the buried things.

Hoping that these chains stay hidden, alas this hope is worthless because the box to which we keep the things buried is flawed. There is always a crack in the containment because things cannot stay dead. Truth has a way of worming its way through any obstacle, sometimes that truth works like a blowtorch, burning through the places that we buried those things. Sometimes in the revelation of these things we find peace, sometimes closure, sometimes redemption and yet sometimes all we find is our hands bound by these very chains, the chains win and we in the end are smothered and suffocated by the things we thought were long defeated.

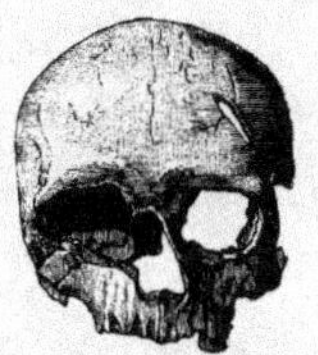

THE DEVILS MOTHER SHRIVELED

FROM THE DIARY OF IVY

As I said, I understand how it was that my mother could not love me. How can you love, when instead of life, bounding and leaping in its effortless stream, instead gives you a brief moment of hope and then. Instead of a cry or a giggle, there in the crib is a corpse. The lifeless body sunken and shaded, what that must have been for her, to see the life she had created, grew and nurtured was now lifeless. She told me once, that her milk still ran long after burning her, and this made it even worse. I can't fathom the humiliation she felt.

By the time I was born, all hope of a healthy child had been ripped from her, she told me later on that she was always afraid we would be next. This fear in her, driving her to abandon instead of protect, consumed by grief. She seems now in reflection more like a specter than a mother. Something that 'was' alive but now a shade, a pale version of 'mother', simply there in the room like the weird clock on the wall or the doily from grandma. She became a fixture of the home and he took her place, and became the loudest center of my world.

I am certain, that I can excuse the yearnings I have by knowing now, what torture that must have been. It is hard to know if I was wanted or loved, how does one know that? We in our stupidity as children toss back vitriolic poison at the things that birthed and made us, we spit back at them hatred, despite the lack of truth in that hate. For me, there was some truth in the bitterness I had, as my parents were not exactly the best at their job, they took punishment too far, often lashing out with spoons or belts.

There in my sanctuary of my room, my solace was only to know that someday I would get free of this. My mother's suffering was felt in her addiction and my childhood was mostly cleaning it up. Cleaning the vomit, the horror, the shit smeared sheets. Explaining away why dinner was not ready, why laundry was not clean. I took on the mantle of mother instead of daughter and child, and there in that place, I kept vigil for the hand that would sweep out from nowhere and strike. Like a viper it would sit there and wait, maybe now, or now, what was it I did again, stupid Ivy, stop putting the sugar bowl in the wrong place, ignorant Ivy, stop forgetting the sheet needs to be straight.

Up again, down again, you're stupid Ivy, you're dumb, you are the worst. Over and over the words I would tell myself. Like a bedtime story they went on and on, from one minute to the next, looping until infinity. My mother at least had her bottle to soothe her, she had the drink to keep her asleep, while I had nothing. She knew what he was, his sickly breath lingered in the house. It felt as if you were a doll in a dollhouse, and he was the cruel master who not just pulled your strings but disjointed your limbs. Burning you with his magnifying light, that twisted and yanked your flesh from its bone. He was evil, she was nothing, there we were alone and frightened and small.

There is something now that I must admit, being small gives one certain advantages. We can run faster, hide better, and can take your hate. We swallow it like liquid, allowing it to shape us into something you cannot touch. We are the monster, the one you created, it's just a matter of whether we will be the good monster or bad one, that is what we cannot see. I knew others that had tried to be good, there was always in me this dream that I had become something else. Maybe in another life, I escaped this hell, and forged myself a life free from pain. Never did I allow anyone to render my flesh raw, maybe I owned my body now, maybe I am a mother, a wife, maybe I am loved, but these delusions are just that.

The unreal dreams of a pathetic little shit that is nothing and no one who is now sitting here wondering to herself if she remembered to clean behind every book. Checking and scanning the room as a cleaning robot seeking out to destroy dirt. In my room, I found solace in the quiet when his breath would not crush me, clinging to my teddy bears I would dream of rescue. The night would come again, and the walls closed in. He would come into the house ready for his inspection. Our father came home his white gloves donned, he proceeded to wipe the house again, walking round every surface, inspecting every surface. He finished, lifting the glove. I knew then my despair would win, and again the vile wretch of me spilled out like water.

I looked at him, knowing that it would be me. I clenched my fist, I refused to give him the sick pleasure of knowing he hurt me, I refused to have my will broken, my body no longer feared him, but reviled him. I was beginning to lose the part of myself that was good, and yet I wanted it lost. I wanted to rip out of me all that was shining and good and decent and turn myself into hate, I wanted to hate him, I wanted to kill him, I wanted to make him suffer. But, instead, because I am nothing and garbage and deserving of his vile nature, my fist gives way, and I surrender to the nature of fear, I cannot help what I am, I cannot change what he is.

“Is this what you call clean?” He snapped, “Get down on your knees you selfish little brat, I will show you”

“No, daddy, not again” I cried, “I cleaned it, I did, I swear, I was up all night, dusting and dusting, ask sister, she will say. She will say” My voice is breaking

The belt undone, he pulls it off and strikes; “Don’t talk back to me, you selfish brat!” He hits, “I will teach you to talk back, calling that clean, you’re disgusting, you’re as bad as your mother, disgusting whores”

The lashing continues, three more, four more, the pain on my back, the pain in her eyes, as I try to not cry out, hoping that he will just tire of me, will he never let me go, and yet, I could not help but feel he enjoyed this. Five more, six, seven. The pain twisting itself into a blissful numbness, all I can think of is escape. I plan it out, I see the window in the room, I imagine myself fleeing. It was her that kept me there, her small dark eyes wishing for this nightmare to stop, feeling my pain, holding her bear.

"STOP HITTING SISTER" my little sister yelled out, "she cleaned it, I saw her"

"Shut up, or it's you next" he snarled

"Run sister run", I said, turning my body so he could not see where she hid. I took the pain for her, like a badge of honor I wore those marks to remind me of him, of this, of my worth.

My sister had a hiding place that only we knew, there we would hide away from the monster in the house. Not even the light would pull him back, in fact nothing would. Nothing stopped the monster in its tracks, he was like a sick unrelenting force that transmuted itself from father to abuser and back again. My mother, where was she? It's funny, how now I don't recall where she was. My memories are not that good for this.

I have tried to block out a lot of this, but you asked for my story and so I am recalling it, like speaking about a nightmare that you had when you were two, the monster remains, but the boundaries of that nightmare have fuzzy edges and who was in that dream is long gone. Memories are odd that way, they are not real pictures of the totality of life, they are like pictures soaked in water, peeled and smeared. They are not a true picture of what was, often obscured and replaced with omission as a way to cope. There inside myself I built a palace to which I could keep my feelings in one box, locked with a key.

There in the real world he could do his worst, but this chest, this box, he could not touch. I would lob myself in front of my younger sister, taking his heat, his anger and more. It was there, as I was crying and sniffling in my room, afraid the monster would find me, even in this most quiet place, he could smell me. Like a fox chasing a rabbit, he knew where I was.

"Come out here Ivy, right now, you little brat, or else it's going to get a lot worse, I am waiting child. You should not have left your towel on the floor, so help me, there is no one as dumb as you child, I am giving you till the count of ten...1...2..."

His counting went on, and I was hoping, and rocking, and hiding my sister behind me. This night would wash away like all the others, and leave in its wake only the wounds, only the pain. Night after night this went on until I became eighteen. It was then I ran. Ran away leaving all of the pain behind. I left my sister there; I could not save her. I was a child, and if I could change anything it would be rescuing her. Time continued on, as if it did not care to stop for a minute and catch its breath, it aged me, I forgot the home I came from. I did what I could to continue on.

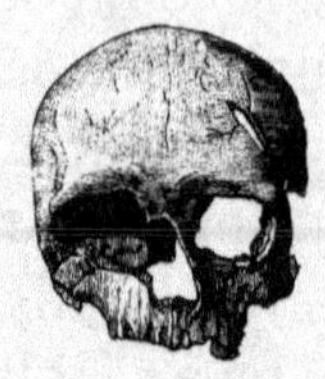

SEX SENT ME TO THE DEVILS BED

I woke up again, the nightmare revisited, I was lying in my apartment above the bakery. The smell of bread wafted into the room. So many years, alone. I recall the trial, I remember what happened, the thing that stole my family. They never found her, and nothing of her remains. There is only this Ivy now. Twisting the cap off the pills again, I make myself Ivy for the day. Getting around the world with these scars is exhausting, but there it is, the sweet smell of coffee lingering through the air. I rise up out of bed, stretch and pet the cat.

"Morning little one", I said, scratching the large fat orange tom cat behind the ears.

I went into the kitchen, off again to the races. I wish my life was as interesting as the shows I watch every night. Then I could be Ivy Malone, FBI, but no. I am just Ivy, a single name etched on a gold-plated name tag at the local corner store. At least there I was not asked many questions about why I didn't have ID. I mean, they don't care, they just needed a girl that looked pretty to run the cash. Something about a pretty girl being less likely to rob.

My boss even encouraged me to dress a little bit, what did he say? 'Revealing'. Slutting myself up in my crushed velvet top that just showed a bit of shoulder, its ripped sleeves showing the pretty tattoo underneath. My tight black jeans showing off my ass like serving up juicy plums on a plate, fit snugly against my skin. Tonight's plan, going to hit that club again. Need a good night out with Manson to get me in the mood to survive the week.

"Isn't that right Shadow", I asked the cat, who just yawned and spread out his claws gearing up for his daily sleep.

Grabbing my keys, shoving the club shirt into the bag hanging there, I prepare myself for the day. Typical city air. The smog crushes my lungs with its weight. The dirt and grime of my cheap low rent building clings onto my canvas vans. What can I do, I don't have I.D. No one around here does, it's our skid row, and skid we do, down streets that we run through instead of walk, cause here is where the monsters live, but we know those monsters don't we Ivy, we know them all too well.

I was not scared of this place. I walk confidently, jumping on bus 85 heading downtown. Shoving some earbuds in my ears, the pumping sounds of Disturbed are my jam today. I try to not lock eyes on the bus drivers, something about a chick dressed like me, garners attention. They love to look don't they, dripping like dogs they sneer at me. So, I play with them. Gently rubbing my leg, biting my ruby stained lip, and smiling, you want me, I will play, come and stare, come and get it, if you dare. Just as the heat in the bus reaches its climax, it stops. I shrug and walk off the bus my juicy plums bouncing in the distance, surely one of those apes is going to enjoy rubbing off to that one. That's you in a nutshell Ivy, a tease, a monster.

"What's up, Ivy, ready for another day at grind" Sam yelled out as I walked in

"Guess, so" I replied, "Is the inventory ready for us to count?"

"Yep, it's all ready to go if you are", Sam said, following me to the back with his clipboard, "No one else is in yet, so we got lots of time, I think the boss has the day off and with it being a holiday and all, we can take our time, won't be anyone comin' in today" he finished, as we headed into the back.

I hated inventory day, but what can you do? I needed the overtime and it's not like I have anyone to invite over anyway, so why not, get paid, put things on shelves, whatever. I roll up my sleeves and begin to unpack items. Sam is there helping; he is a good guy. Staring at my shirt he smiles. A few boxes bump into my chest as he grabs them, I feel his hands slowly brush against me, but it's OK. I kind of want him to. Maybe I want him to do more. He looks so hot in that outfit today, I tie back my hair, showing my neck. Play Ivy, turns again, biting her lip and showing a little bit more skin. Sam smiles, the next time reaching a little closer, until on one hand off he drops the bag of rice.

It smashes all over the floor and he grabs me and begins kissing me, his lips feel moist and deeply fused to mine. It's so hot, and the urge to devour him there and then sweeps over me. I feel myself stripping off the crushed velvet revealing the pair of plump breasts hidden behind a dark lacy bra. His hands feel around for the clasps, he tastes good. My mind is slipping, the memories of the first rape slide back into my mind. Flashes of pain, of sadness, of his hands grabbing at my skirt, ripping flesh and crying.

My father again, flashes of him spitting the words of "slut, whore, useless" drifting from his mouth. The flashes give way to the smell of him, the now, the present. It is always like this. Those of us who are fractured live and exist in two worlds. One is that which we exist in and inhabit, the other is the palace of secrets to which we keep and preserve the pain. Rape does not mean we will never enjoy the pleasures of flesh; it is a delicate balance like juggling a knife on your head. You can shove away that pain and not feel it as your pleasure takes hold, it is possible. Still every lover I have had and there have been many, were more a way to avoid dealing with my pain, like the pills.

Sex was like a drug that I could use, it took me over, and brought me semblance of love, a moment in which I could be lost in the flesh of a lover, seeing their purity, reminding myself I was still worthy, even if it was just for this. The hunger takes over. I want him, I want him to destroy me. Take it, take it all, this shedding of the light, it feels so good to give in, give over. The meds obviously aren't keeping her back, I feel my body shift harder, pushing him down, I mount him and ride his pleasure back and forth in waves. Like an animal I grunt, and squeal, he pinches my breast, and slaps my plump ass. He feels so good, and then it's over. Picking up my clothing, I slip back on my underwear and fix my shirt.

"Well" Sam coughs, "Not sure what I am supposed to.."

"Nothing", I reply, "I don't want anything from you, in fact, I would rather you don't tell anyone about this.."

"Ok, cool, cool. Can I at least walk you home?" He asks

"Sure, why not" I reply, grabbing up my stuff.

Sam grabbed the broom, sweeping up all the rice, I went back to business, just putting the last few items on the shelf. Sam tries not to look at my body. The voice is there, she is hungry to get out, and to let him know he should run now, run before I am not myself, one never knows what that means. The memories, they bleed into the now. My eyes pale and there it is again, the darkness, the other her, she is sitting there rocking back and forth, holding onto the bed.

"Best not tell your daddy about this" the boy says, "Wouldn't want him to know his little darling is a whore"

Sobbing, "I want to go home"

"Of course, hm , juicy little slut like you better clean up first though, don't want daddy to know I was inside you, hm, fucking sweet little virgin pussy. Get dressed, before I do it again"

Slumping, I grab my clothing, he touches my face, and I feel him twisting my wrist, "You're hurting me..."

"This, this is nothing. Remember I know where you live. Remember you let me in. Remember I could do terrible things to you Ivy, terrible things"

"I remember, I promise, I won't tell"

He lets me go smelling my hair as I leave. This is not the worst that happens, this is just another day in the life of Ivy, another day where my body is not my own, when my own being is owned by another man, twisted and dark, I turn from the safe and innocent lamb, into the dirt and grime of the worm. I am the worm now, the monster now, I am responsible for this, but how did he know.

"You slut!" My daddy yelled, "What good are you!!", "Who's going to marry some whore who can't keep her legs closed"

"He raped me daddy, it was not my fault" I scream back, trying to assess how he knew.

"Doesn't matter, its your fault, walking with that dress, stupid slut" his hand slaps me again, my face going red, but this was before I had you to protect me. So I took it, over and over again.

The boy sitting there for dinner for three years, his hands drifting on my lap, grabbing and grabbing at me. Trying to get away, trying to get help, and only facing eyes of judgment, eyes of disappointment, you're the whore here, your the slut here, it's your fault, it's your fault. Snapping back to the now, I wipe the tears off, trying to remember the mantra. If you just think about the now Ivy, recalling my therapy. Breathe, breathe, mantra after mantra, calm down...3...2...1...Sam grabs his coat, and we head to the door, switching off the lights we head out up North to the bus stop, being a decent guy, he lets me on first, even pays my fare. We get off at my stop, he walks me up to my place.

"Thanks for um. Walking me" I say, kind of blushing

"No problem" he replies, putting his hands on my door frame, he slumps in for a kiss

I comply, of course I do. I am sure your thinking, do rape victims like sex? What a dumb question, of course I do. Rape didn't destroy me, but it did change me. I see sex as a must, something I have to give, because my body is not my own. There is something in this acceptance that is sharply aware of the irony. Rape is taking away your power, and for me, it did. I had no power to say no.

Even though Sam is not the vile monster that twisted me, he is a symbol of a thing I must give into, that no one is barred from the secret hidden nature of my flesh. It was not love, it was an act, an act of compliance, of submission and of the truth in one singular fact.

I have no ownership of my body. I turn to unlock the door, and Sam approaches from behind, he presses against me. Unlocking the door, he grabs my ass, I turn and look at him, he walks towards me, lifts me up and closes the door.

"I want to eat you up Ivy" he whispers

He lays me down, and blissfully kisses every inch of me. I feel him penetrate me, his fingers thrusting deep inside, wave after wave of orgasm drips from my cup, slathering him with blissful sticky honey. He is grunting now, kissing me harder and harder, he moves to my breast, gently kissing and sucking, the flow of ecstasy is flooding the mattress, I feel so wet, so embarrassed and yet he just is riding the waves, enjoying watching every twitch. I try to touch him, his hand pushes me down, he just wants me. Just me to feel this right now. So, I let him, and hours float by and he is simply giving. His face dives deep between my thighs, he licks at my fleshy mounds with deep lust. I feel myself writhing. He lives in this space for what seems like hours, I am enjoying this, and so is he. His rock-hard cock presses against my thighs. He wants all of me, every inch and when I cannot take anymore, he finally looks at me.

"I want to fuck you now"

"Yes...Sam....please"

There was a time in this frozen landscape that Sam was my fire in the darkness. The months together were amazing, he was amazing, but I couldn't give him the one thing he wanted. He can have my flesh, that's free but my soul is not just mine. Come on Ivy, get it together, just put the shirt on, the makeup on and go, he doesn't need to see the damaged broken doll underneath. I think it was what drove him away, who knows really. They all leave in the end. Too bad it was not meant to be.

It's been months now since Sam was at the store, I guess like all the others they just come for a while and are gone, never with me for long. Although I can't recall how it ended now, it doesn't matter though. It's just the end of one chapter, and on to the next. The days went on at the corner store, I worked hard and earned my way, not even having had to give away any more of Ivy. I wondered sometimes if I should find Sam, but what's the point, he got his. Still the sound of spilled rice in the back brings me to that wonderful day, and for feeling of him against me.

There's been a few in between. Some good, some bad, some left marks. Whatever, what else could I do, they own me, right? The pills were helping again, it was quiet again, the feelings were not so cold. I had earned the day off, deciding to take myself up to the museum. Got myself all dolled up to head off and enjoy the day, sporting a tight white t-shirt and blue jeans. Taking the bus up to the East side of the city. The leering eyes on the bus starring again, let them. Getting off the bus, I head in, finding myself in my favorite room again. Something about dinosaurs just fascinates me. Wandering around, I find my favorite bench right in front of T-Rex when this gorgeous blonde in tight jeans and a Bowie t-shirt wanders over and plops herself beside me. I smiled at her and she smiled right back, there was something twinkling about her. She smelled good.

"Names Destiny, what's yours beautiful"

"Ivy", I replied

"Don't suppose a young thing like you wants to join me for a coffee by chance?" She asks

"Sure, why not?" I replied

"Sweet, I am parked right outside, we can go down to one of those places by the pier, maybe we can hang out and get to know each other"

I am sure the lecture of 'don't go with strangers' is playing as loudly in your head as it is mine, but she seemed safe to me. I felt it was OK and anyways, what's the worst that's going to happen, I have had it all happen to me, and she smelt nice. We headed out of the museum and jumped in her red Volvo.

Destiny flipped on the radio to Sound of Silence by Disturbed and off we went, rocking away to the sounds that blasted out of speakers.

"Nice", I thought to myself, "She's into Disturbed, might actually be a cool chick"

Arriving at the coffee shop, we head in, and Destiny and I grab a big cup of coffee and sit down. The view at this place is stunning, it was beautiful out, the ocean a few feet from the window. Out in the waves, you could see boats sailing out and in, the smooth motion of the world in the free world of the ocean. The salty air wafted through sheer curtains that flanked the outdoor patio. We just sat there in this silence, almost healing from whatever wounds we had. It was as if we were in this retreat on some distant place, and any minute now we would emerge different.

"So, get into strangers' cars often?" Destiny asked smiling

"No" I laughed, "Not usually, but you seemed OK"

Destiny laughed, "Well, I mean, not like you can tell right, I could be a psycho"

We both burst out laughing. I wouldn't want to ruin it for her, but she's the one that should be afraid.

"So, what you do for a living" Destiny inquired, sipping the white cup

"Oh, me?" I replied, "I work down at Discount Mart as a cashier, nothing important really"

"Meh, a job is a job." She says smiling, she was trying to make me feel equal and that was something I really appreciated

"You?" I asked

"I work down ye olde DMV, processing licenses, not exactly glamorous either" she says, shrugging

We sit still and silent a minute or two longer, our cups empty and our bellies full, she looks at me in this way to say, what are you? As if trying to see the thing beneath my eyes. She is searching for an answer, but instead just stares at me, and I get lost in her eyes. It doesn't seem long before her hand wanders over the table and holds mine. She smiles and I bite my lip. My heart flutters as she strokes my fingers gently with hers, she smells good.

She playfully slaps my hand and we get up and head to the car. Diving into the red Volvo she just leaps over the center and it's on. Clothing flying everywhere she is just so soft and juicy. She kisses my neck, holds me, and reaches into my jeans, I am totally into her, I want her more than I want anything. We cut it short to drive to her place and she gets out and opens the door, we run into the building as if we can't get there fast enough.

She unlocks her door and we head to the bed. She tosses me onto the soft white bed, and we drip into each other like water into a pool. She penetrates me over and over with her smooth soft fingers. I allow her to take me into her mouth, I devour her gently and softly. She makes me feel alive. This is the safest I have ever been, she is peaceful. The night lends itself to the morning, and I wake with her hand around me.

"Morning beauty," she says, sweeping my hair away from my face

"Morning," I said

Destiny sat up, stretching herself like a cat. "How about we go out for breakfast and then we take you home and maybe we can hang out a bit more, and maybe we can get to know each other a little bit better." She giggled, slapping my ass on the way out of bed. I followed, getting dressed, we hopped back into her car and drove back to my place. Destiny kept touching my leg. Parking back in front of my place she got out, opened my door and up we went giggling. The nights spent in my room were ones I will remember forever fondly. A few nights before Halloween, I had gotten off early to take Destiny out to the club, arriving at her place. I heard a noise from outside her door. Groaning, sighing.

"Yes. Yes, lick it. Harder, oh my god," was heard outside the thin metal door, I remember opening the door and that's why I saw them. Destiny wrapped up in the thighs of a red-headed girl, her gaping hole oozing with fluid. She was riding Destiny's face.

Then cold, it went cold again, so dark it is here, what is this? What is this? I felt the cold sting of rejection, I walked out of her apartment, I closed the door. Another chapter for me, I guess, another wound to carry, another world in which I could in fact be myself again. The days bleed into each other, got to remember to get a refill on those pills. My life moved on. I found myself wondering when I would be OK again, when my heart would love again. This is when my visions got worse. I recalled again what was broken inside. I felt myself lost in a world like Alice, I dropped into a hole that I don't feel I can escape. I am inside this hell, I know, I need it over. I grab the knife, this time the monster takes it. I slice deep into my wrist. It's over, it's over. The next memory is white. White coats, all over me. I feel the bandages, I wake up.

"No, I was supposed to"

"Be dead", the man says, the man in the white coat looks at me with anger

"Almost were but they found you in time, there is always another way little girl, always"

"How would you fucking know, this was supposed to be it", I sobbed

"I know you're hurting right now, but it will get better, we will make you better", he said, tapping on the IV line

"Where am I?" I said

"The Satsujin Asylum" he replied

The walls surround me, I feel the cold floor, touching my skin. I hear in the hall the clacking of heels. I recall cold, wet, something flashing, why can't I remember what it was that happened. I cannot see the night before, it's gone, it's just gone. A memory slips in. It was with the boys from school again, there was dirt, ground, a doll. What is going on? Why can't I think straight? There is light streaming in from the barred windows, the light shines on my hands.

They don't look like my hands though, they are sunken and dirty, weathered and old. It feels like I have aged, wasted away in here, forgotten and locked away. I remember the humming, the sweet humming of a boy who stroked my hair, the feeling of him holding me, but it seems like this is just a dream. Just a dream. Why is it so hard to recall? What is this place? I feel around to find where i am, but there is only metal and the smell of piss and shit, I hear them in the hall, clicking their heels on the floor, there is a small window in the door, it opens sometimes, someone looks in.

They come in, shove me down, I wrench my body hard, but to no use, the pills go in, the darkness, the cold. Another day dawns. It seems they bleed out from one to the next, the sunlight, the moonlight, it's all the same. The door, the lock, the keys, the wrenching, the spitting, the needle, the pills. Round and round it goes. That is until I met the doctor. He was tall, sturdy, always seemed to enjoy shoving in a needle deep into my vein. The man in the coats came to pull me into his office, lifted and rushed through the hallways, don't look at the others, keep your eyes down, otherwise they will hit you, they will hurt you, be good Ivy, be good.

They bring me in and place me on a bed securing my arms to the rails, he gives me that uncomfortable look of a monster about to devour me. My gown is sheer and opens slightly revealing my sullen skin. My breasts were no longer perky and pink, but wasted away from the lack of sun and nutrients. They were no longer just "toys for boys", or the things that feed babies, they were something gray and worn. It didn't stop him though, it didn't stop him from grabbing them, and pinching my nipples.

"Like that, little girl" he whispered, "I bet you do, I can see how much you like it, getting all wet down there", his hand slid downward finding my pussy and rubbing my clit with intense passion.

I try to hide the moans, he stops, looks deeply in my eyes and said, "Not yet, I want to make you wait"

He covers up my flesh, and sits down, with his pad in hand. "Now then, lets begin again, the last time we spoke, you mentioned you know why your here"

"Yes, I think so, although it's still a bit foggy and still lost."

"So, you don't know why you're here then?" He says, taking off his glasses and folding them neatly, placing them in the right pocket

I struggled to think, to remember, what was it, there was something, some flash, liquid, breathing, a smell, dirt, blood, screaming. What was it? Damn you Ivy, remember for god's sake. I lifted my head and looked at him, almost begging for an answer, until I only managed to squeak out a tiny little stupid set of words that rolled out of me in desperation.

"So, I am cracked then?"

"Yep, completely"

"Nice...", "Was wondering when that would happen"

"Don't suppose you want to get better?" He asks

"Don't know if you can fix me doc, I am fucked up" I replied, crying

"Well aren't we all", he replied, "Tell you what, you give me a chance and I promise I will help you get out of those bindings" he pointed at the cuffs securing me to the bed

I bit my lip, as his hands caressed my legs, of course, of course Ivy. Just spread your legs, give him what he wants.

"Oh, not yet. I want to teach you something. How to be better at your skills. I want to teach you how to be me." He said

I look at him, his eyes show the story of a monster lying in wait. There is where I met the first man to whom my body would belong to, it was there that I found myself again in that silent place, hoping and waiting for it to end, he would hit me, when I deserved it. My ripped dress there on the floor again, my body hunched and racked with pain, as this time he got rough, he was my everything, my all, and I worshiped him. The dark Ivy disappeared into the calm and suppressed Ivy, ready to surrender her soul again to his fist, or his large member that would force itself into my openings whenever and whenever they wanted. It was there in the whimpering corner that I would calm myself. On the couch again, this time my cuffs off now, and left to the wayside.

"Do you remember the night it happened?" He asked, "Tell me, how it felt to take his life, and spare no detail" the doctor said, slipping his hands deep into my panties, wet again, he always made me wet

"He betrayed me" I whimpered, "I took the knife, I remember it felt heavy in my hand, breathing heavy, I cut him" I replied, whimpering and shivering with ecstasy at the cum leaking down my leg.

He takes his hand up, and shoves his fingers into my mouth, "Lick it off for me baby, lick that sweet juice off me, that's it, so pretty, your mouth is so sweet, want to fuck me now baby, hm?" He asks, whisking his pants off with his free hand, to reveal a huge erect cock waiting for me.

I stand, rip off my wet panties, and straddle his cock with my pussy, I ride him until we both finish, slumping into each other, he kisses me deeply and reaches down to continue rubbing my swollen clit.

"Not done with you yet little girl" the doctor continued, lifting me off him, turning me and taking me from behind, I feel his hard cock pounding me over and over, and the memories of the blood of the death, why? Why now.

ꕥ

The next session, it's winter now, and the leaves are long dead, the doctor and I sharing the secrets I held so deep within, he knows me now, deeply knows, and he holds in him the secrets I carried, and buried.

"You know that I won't tell them where you buried him right? He says, zipping up his pants

"I know, you won't, but you do have to let me out of here someday, and,"

"Yeah, and I will hold your secrets my dear, as you have held mine"

He told me of the times in his youth when his mother would hit him with belts, and rub his cock with her hand, he told me the sick and twisted tale of his mother's lips kissing him. He told me of how the day came where he could not take it anymore, and where she was buried.

He told of the other women who he loved, and tried to love, and how they too betrayed him, and where they now were laid to rest. He told of how he learned to hide what he was, becoming 'respectable', and he showed me how to poison, how to hide the stench of the bodies, he showed me how to kill, how to twist the knife. He was not a good doctor, he was definitely a bad one, a hidden twisted psycho in a white coat, but aren't they all? Seriously, medicine seems closer to perverted and twisted humans who just want to have the right to your body, it's not a 'do no harm' profession as they keep telling me, it's a 'lets see the inside of that' 'thing" situation.

The months bleed into each other, the time seems to be filled with these sessions, my cell, the world just drifted on. I was beginning to want out, beginning to desire to exit, this time not the way in which I entered this place, but, to run. Run far away, far away from the 'bad doctor', far away from these dreams, he was getting too close, too close to knowing me. The next session began.

"Are you going to tell me, what happened that day?" He asked

This time the session was being watched by a group of student doctors, so his pants stayed straight, his composure was serious, straight and professional.

"I can't..." I cried, "I don't remember, I don't remember" screaming for this to stop, as the shocks would come, then his questions, then more, the pain was incredible, I could not take much more.

Tears rolled down from my face, I was begging him with my eyes, begging him to make it stop. The months went on still and I began to learn how to hide what I am, I began to convince him to let me go. "If I was free, we could do more of the things you enjoy." I offer, sitting up on his desk, opening my gown to reveal my shaved pussy.

He leans down his head and licks my clitoris, I moan with extreme pleasure as he shoves his fingers in, until I push back his head.

"I am going to stop giving you this unless you let me free."

I get up from the desk and walk out. It did not take long until my papers were prepared, he got me a little den apartment near his, he visited me everyday, and I began to change myself to be more hidden, but it was time wasn't it. It was time to hide the past, and that meant cleaning up a few loose ends. It was Valentines Day, when I showed up at his apartment, dressed in a little two piece baby doll negligee. He opened the door to let me in, he picked me up, and we fucked on every surface of the room. Over and over he would toss me on a counter, feverishly lapping up my cum, fucking me over and over again, until I spilled all the fluids within all over him.

The floors were covered with puddles of joy. In a moment of rest, as the 'bad doctor' went to go clean up, I noticed on the counter my file, it was not that fact alone that got under my skin, but it was seeing that in this file, was pictures of not just me, but me and the 'others' and there was a note with a file of another girl. Her hair was sandy blonde, her eyes held the secrets like mine once did, they were innocent, and I saw his notes, that were the same as mine.

He was grooming her too, in me I felt a pain I had forgotten, there was a thing in me that grew, the heat of the anger began to burn into me, rising, growing. There was something about seeing her, that hit like a light-bulb. I don't recall exactly how it happened, but I know I used the bottle that he showed me before. I know I measured a thing, stirred a thing, got his glass of scotch ready, I was waiting for him. Waiting there in on the table, my legs spread open, revealing him my dripping wet pussy, he looked at me as if I was a prime rib, he wanted to devour me, I knew that.

He walked over, he took the drink I handed him, and shot it down in one gulp, tossed the glass, and let it shatter on the floor, before he knelt down to service me once more, and then, it was quiet. He was there, slumped on the floor, stone dead. I got up, grabbed his medical pass and got to work. I got dressed, cleaned up, and got the bleach, the sunlight streamed into the apartment, revealing a beautiful and grotesque scene of shining silver and concrete mixed with a slowly decomposing corpse. I then went out and grabbed a big laundry cart from the apartment, went back and grunted while lifting his body inside.

They don't tell you how heavy a body is. I mean you would think he weighed as much as a tank, but he weighed more than that, so it took me a bit to get his body in there. I wheeled it down covered by laundry and took it to a place that I knew he would never be found. Down in the dark I flipped my switchblade open and went to work and tried to make the body more manageable. Getting him into the laundry bin was hard enough.

Now I had to get him out of the building and buried somehow. It was frustrating to say the least. God damn switchblade wasn't enough to cut through the stringy sinew and tendons of his joints. It was making my hands ache and making me mad. I finally lost it, angry rage boiled up from deep inside me and I started stabbing out of pure frustration. Stupid but there it was, primal rage. In the end I had to drag the body and it took awhile. Burying it was surprisingly, the easy part.

From there, I went to the clinic, swiping his card to get into his office, and destroyed every piece of the Ivy he knew, he recorded, he made note of. Luckily he had written me down as Jane Doe, and no one would ever know I was 'Ivy". They will never find him, not where I left him, and no one will know will they Ivy, no one will know.

It was this one act that turned me for the last time. The Ivy I was...finally gone, here in the darkness, my palace of secrets burnt to the ground. The past melted away and there was only now. I took a shower and mopped up every corner of that bastards apartment. Wiping his bits off the knife, dumped out the remaining liquid, wrapped up the evidence, as the knife glistened in my hand.

I wrapped my face with a mask and took the bleach to scrub with vigor, the entire apartment. Sweating and laboring, I took no breaks. I scrubbed the walls, the floors, the bed, everything. When I left, you would have never known that I was there, and I made sure none ever saw me coming or going. No one would ever hurt me again, that much I knew. When I look back on the times, I gave myself excuses to let them hurt me.

Why was I unworthy of love, what is it that I have so desperately been running from. Here in the darkness in the 'after' I sit and wonder what it was to feel pain. My bones know no memory of it, they do not recall what it was that twisted me or what it was that turned me to him. It hardly matters now does it. Hasn't it been so that this broken doll was always thus. She was both evil and good, both dark and light. There in some ways I have learned what it is that made me. I am the creation of monsters, I am the darkness, I am the slave, the slut, the whore.

It is my knife that finds itself seeking you out, for they are not all vessels of my father, of Sam, of Destiny, they are the shadows of those that inflicted and racked pain upon me. Each flick of my blade was a mark of that which I have endured, you deserve it no doubt, I am sure. Everyone is the one who didn't help us, everyone is the one who never listened, so come closer, let me tell you again. I am Ivy, and I am waiting, come closer and let me share with you my love, my lust, my death. Become my lover, my sister, my all, I am the monster you have longed for, and I am hungry for more.

I found the place in the dark corners of the web and once again took an identity unto my own. Ivy I was again, but this Ivy would be a dark and twisted one. I found myself in the pharmacy, digging for some hair dye. Let's go with midnight black, I said to myself. I grabbed up some Gothic eyeliner, black dark pallets of swirling metal and dark charcoals. I took it to the doctors pad, why not? Down with the old Ivy and up with the dark Ivy.

I took the dye, and removed any trace of the former me, the dark lines of thick cat eyes replaced my demure soft palate of pastels. The streaks of black across my eyes, the dark deep pool of black polish surrendered my white nails to the night. I vamped up the lips, I ripped my shirt, slashed my pants, and to add to it all, I took a small knife and cut into my skin some little tattoo marks.

I was now reborn. Slipping on the doctors old docs completed the ensemble, his feet were only a half size bigger than mine. It's not true what they say about feet, for his feet disguised the wide heavy meat that hung from his legs, his penis was mighty big, mighty meaty, and I had engorged myself upon him like a kid consuming their favorite chocolate.

Cleaning up the apartment, I made sure I wiped it all down with bleach, I walked out, locked the door, and slipped the key in the bag full of trash. See ya in hell, I thought as I slipped out in the dead of night and found myself wandering once again the dead eyes of those haunted dolls lingering in my mind, here I was again you fuckers, this time, I am pissed.

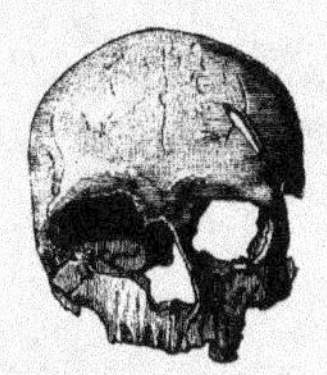

THE NEOPHYTE MISSED THE MARK

Leo stood there in the trampled grass staring. The grass around him was tamped down. He was brooding, lost in thought while baring his teeth aggravated at the complete shit show this had become. The body had been male. John Doe was torn up, cut up and partly in pieces. It looked like he'd been there awhile at the secondary dump scene. The local wildlife had a field day with the body and parts were missing. Mostly fingers and toes, chewed up bits of flesh from buttocks to thighs.

The body had been dragged from the primary dump scene. Something their perp hadn't anticipated would happen it seemed. Bast was yelling at some of the C.S.I team members, also greenhorns, for traipsing around the damn place like little ballerinas, mucking up evidence that they couldn't get back now. That was Leo's fault. He hadn't taken proper charge of the crime scene. He'd messed up. He was furious, not at the team but at himself. It was a massive under sight on his part and he knew better.

Now, he would pay for the mistake and might pay with his budding career on the table. Ari approached cautiously, taking a wide berth around Leo toward the other end of the circle of grass he was standing in. The body was in a body bag in the middle of the grass. Loose parts of the body stuffed in with it. Ari frowned, that wasn't normal for a crime scene processing. They usually left the body until the pictures were done and samples were taken. She was crouched down, looking up at the man next to her. Watching him brood angrily.

"So, what next Leo?" She asked as gently as she could. He had a temper and he knew how to damn well show it too.

Sometimes a little too well. He'd never put his hands on her, or anyone for that matter, but she'd seen him get close to it once. Only once.

"I lose my job, maybe, for fuck sake. What do you think is next Ari?" He spat back at her, winced then looked at her sheepishly, "I'm sorry darlin'. I didn't mean to shout at you baby girl."

Leo turned back to the body, contemplating the score marks, the chewed bits, and the leftovers of the scene. He hung his head. Gods, what a mess this was. The marks on the body that weren't from animals looked like some sort of knife at a cursory look. Not a big one it seemed but one that was big enough to be used to try to reduce the body into more manageable parts. A partially failed attempt as it were but it gave them at least something forensically to go on if it wasn't a common knife. If it was common, like a kitchen knife or a mass produced switchblade Leo and the team were screwed.

There was no outwardly evidence of how John Doe died. No stab marks that indicated ante mortem wounds, but definitely postmortem wounds. No GSR wounds either, which led Leo to suspect he may have been poisoned somehow but that was Ari's department then. The stab marks were frenzied, angry, vicious postmortem stabbings. Well into the thirties or forties for count. Quite the passionate stabber we have here. Leo's eyes roamed around the body, through the grass, any evidence that had been left behind, if any, had been thoroughly trampled and destroyed. No boot print marks, no samples, what little they would glean from this scene would come from John Doe himself.

Leo did see that the body had likely been dragged by animals from whatever area it had been hidden in though. Little bits of evidence that it had, though trodden on, were evident here and there, it fit with the fact body parts were missing and chewed to bits as well. Means whoever killed this poor sap didn't bury the body deep enough for the animals to not get at him. It meant that likely, his perp was a novice killer or it was pure emotional rage with an opportunity to kill presenting itself to the killer.

It was a primal kill they were looking at. Could mean they may have a budding serial killer on their hands. One that was evolving, one that was practicing their new found skills. Leo was sure they would see an escalation and a timeline that would jump rapidly into a possible killing spree.

ꕤ

"So, you let the C.S.I team trample your scene, secondary albeit and you didn't follow the chain of evidence either?" Bast growled at her underling sitting before the inquiry panel.

"That's right. I screwed up. It's on me, not them. I was supervising the team as team leader and it's my fault the case is a cold case now." Leo grunted through gritted teeth.

"Tell me about the rest of the evidence, what you do have Agent Desbrates." Another panel member asked. She was a short woman, blonde and blue eyed. Soft spoken but he had been warned that she could be fierce as well, if you overstepped your boundaries with her that is.

"Well, Ari, the coroner, had determined he'd been poisoned and that was the cause of death. The poison was tetrahydrozoline. It's found in eye drops used to reduce redness of the eyes. In the right amount it can induce a heart attack but leaves the system with only trace amounts left behind. You'd have to be looking for it to know it was there. It was pure fluke that we found the source of the poison. As for the cuts and gashes, they were post mortem with some sort of blade, we determined it was possibly a common switchblade, that left us with nothing to track down. A dual fold reason for the cuts and gashes were what we suspected. One was anger and a primal rage, the other was to try and reduce the body down to a manageable amount to move. Which leads us to suspect the killer likely is female or on the smaller, more effeminate side of male. Likely female though as we found vaginal fluids on John Doe that were missed by the bleach used to clean the body and likely the primary crime scene. It would make our killer a charm and harm killer likely. I, at first thought it may be an evolving serial killer who was escalating; however, I was wrong. There has been no other activity that matches this case anywhere within the radius of the body being found or otherwise and no new leads either. It's a dead case at this time sitting in the cold case files. Also my fault."

"Can you please step out Agent Desbrates, we need to deliberate on how to handle this. We will call you back in when we've come to a conclusion on how we are going to." A dark haired man stated firmly. The third panel member for the inquiry. Leo nodded in his direction and stood up. Walking out of the room while the three panel members started whispering at the table behind him.

"Hey, how'd it go?" Ari said quietly on the bench just outside the door.

"I don't know Ari, I could likely be relieved of my station. They are probably going to ask for my badge and gun at this point. I took all the blame. It's mine to carry that blame." Leo whispered back as he closed the door to the meeting room.

"I'm sorry Leo. I know how much this job means to you."

Leo hung his head, taking a deep sighing breath and when he looked up to look down the hall these green eyes met his. It startled him, she had dark hair, she was petite and dainty. She seemed familiar somehow. She walked by him, looked him dead in the eyes and smiled softly, then walked right past him and turned the corner.

"That was odd wasn't it Leo?" Ari mused, "You know her?"

"No. Yes. Maybe, I don't know."

cs

He'd been lucky that day. They'd determined that while he had messed up they were not going to take his badge but did take his gun from him. They had also determined it was bad enough to leave a black mark in his personnel files and pull him from field work. He could live with that he supposed, not like he had a choice right? Since then, he had become hyper vigilant. By the book as it were.

The mistakes he'd made with the asylum case were haunting him to this very day. It had caused strife between him and Ari, destroying the relationship they had been nursing between them. He'd become obsessed with the asylum case. Especially after finding out the John Doe was a doctor from the nearby looney bin. Dr. Brenner had been a long time psychologist from Satsujin Asylum.

The asylum had been founded by the Sato family who had immigrated to the area post Pearl Harbor era. They had founded the asylum as a refuge for immigrants after the camps had been shut down. They found his files on several dozen women spanning back decades. He had been grooming them sexually and psychologically. His notes had gone from coherent to abhorrent and vile. It had started off with notes you'd typically see from a psychologist about their patients to ratings on how well each woman pleasured him to how susceptible and moldable they were compared to each other.

Which one he might be able to use to his advantage compared to which one might need more "therapy" to coerce them. There were gaps, like some files had been missing somehow but it couldn't be proven and the sick fuck was dead. Leo figured one of his girls, dolls as he called them, may have likely killed him. Coerced him into letting her out and killed him at the closest opportunity she had.

It was a running theory really, Leo didn't have enough evidence to pull the file from the cold case pile besides they'd forbidden him from ever touching the case again. He was barred from it. These days, all Leo had was his academy teaching position, he'd been pulled out of the field for some time to teach instead. They called it a break from field work, he called it punishment for fucking up. Leo looked over his notes for the next lecture he was set to give this week while pounding back last night's Pad Thai.

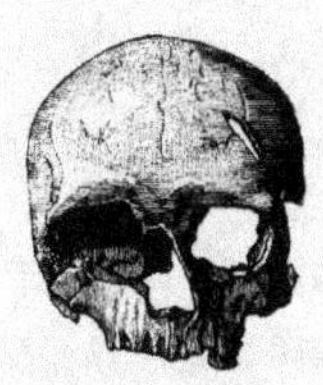

RAPPING. RAPPING SOFTLY AT MY DOOR

Leo looked across the classroom and noted the fresh young faces of the students in front of him. There was a time he was one of those fresh faces. He was dreading this class right to the last minute. He really didn't want to do it, he hated crowds and what Ari called "peopling". He was acutely aware of the stares from the students as he stood there, staring back quietly at them. Gritting his teeth he began,

"Good morning students. This is Forensic Science 101. Today we are looking at the most infamous case that ever graced Scotland Yard." Leo looked around again, they hung on every word he was saying. Every syllable. Leo grunted, he'd forgotten to introduce himself, damn it.

"I'm Leo Desbrates and we are going to examine none other than Jack the Ripper or what we refer to as The Whitechapel Murders. We will examine the victimology, the possible motives, and profile Ripper himself, shall we begin?"

"Wait!"

Leo glanced up from his case notes and files to follow the sound of the female voice. A small petite woman, dark haired with green eyes staring back at him. Those green eyes took his breath away for a moment, they felt familiar somehow. Why did this tiny little thing of a woman feel as if he knew her intimately. She felt like some sort of connection to something he couldn't quite put his thumb on.

"What is it?" Leo responded with irritation at the interruption.

"What's the point of beating a dead horse, the Jack the Ripper case can never be solved." The dark-haired woman replied equally as annoyed.

"Well, for one, we can absolutely learn from the case. Whether it was solved, not solved or unsolvable. Another reason to beat the dead horse is to learn the victimology of the Jack the Ripper case, how the serial killer may have become one and what his profile would look like compared to modern day profiles of serial killers. For example, Ted Bundy for one. Jack the Ripper is the prototype of the Ted Bundys of the world after all."

She seemed satisfied with his answer as the other students muttered approval and nodded in excitement. He smirked; he had to admit, it was a good question. Quick on the smarts this green-eyed beauty in the front row. She was staring at him as if she knew him, again making him feel as if he knew her intimately somehow too. Leo shook it off, nodded back at the class and began his lecture as he riffled through his notes nervously.

Let's start with the victimology shall we. There were five victims, or at least that's the going theory. The last victim doesn't actually fit the victimology, but we'll get to that soon enough. We also have a theory that Mary Ann "Polly" Nichols wasn't Jack the Ripper's first victim. Some speculate that Martha Tabrum was his first victim and that there were two more victims, Alice McKenzie and Frances Coles. Let's meet the victims first.

"The widely accepted first victim was Mary Ann "Polly" Nichols," Leo started as he handed out the booklets on the first five victims, "the other four are Annie Chapman, Elizabeth Stride, Catherine Eddowes and Mary Jane Kelly. Let's begin by looking at their victimology shall we."

DF001-3.d

Langley - F.B.I.
Victimology 101-b
Instructor: Leo Desbrates

Jack the Ripper
How Victimology Plays a Part in Profiling.

Material Resource:
The Mammoth Book of Jack The Ripper Edited by Maxim Jakubowski and Nathan Braund

VICTIM PAPERS

Name: Mary Ann Nichols
Age: 43 years old
Height: 5'2"
Description: Dark hair, grey eyes, front teeth missing teeth. High cheekbones, scar on forehead from childhood accident.

Time of death: August 31st 1888

Post Mortem
1 September 1888

Bruise on the right side of the face and circular one on the left side of the neck. Looked to be thumb and finger placed in a manner to steady the head to lacerate the throat of the victim. Two cuts, both started on the left side of neck below the ear and ran below the jaw. One 4 inches the other 8 inches. Both cuts reached through to the vertebrae. Large vessels of the neck on both sides severed. No other injuries to the upper body.
A sharp, straight object, purported to be a knife was thrust into the lower part of the abdomen, creating a 2-3 inch deep wound from the left side, running jagged. Tissues cut through, several cuts across the abdomen, 3-4 similar running downwards on the right side.
All the wounds\cuts caused by the same instrument, a moderately sharp, long-bladed knife.

Conclusions drawn about the killer:

- Killer is left-handed, attacked Nichols from the front.
- The mutilations took about 4 to 5 minutes to complete and the work of someone with a rough anatomical knowledge.

Name: Annie Chapman
Age: 47 years old
Height: 5'0"
Description: Brown, dark hair, blue eyes, 2 teeth missing. Thick nose, plump, fair complexion. Black eye and bruises on her chest from a recent fight with another woman, Eliza Cooper. Malnourished and diseased with a lung/brain membrane (meningitis?). Disease that would have killed her if our perp had not gotten to her first.

Time of Death: September 8th, 1888

Post Mortem
8 September 1888

Note: Body was stripped and washed by nurses. Shed was unsanitary. Contaminates likely present.

At first sight, the tongue and face were swollen. The throat sliced from left to right through to the spine. A fresh bruise over the temple and over the upper eyelid. Two distinct bruises the size of a man's thumb on the forepart of the top of the chest and on the right hand. By bruising, it is likely that the killer held Chapman by the lower jaw when he cut her throat.
The abdomen had been opened and the intestines cut from their attachments, lifted out and placed on the ground above the right shoulder.
Part of the stomach and a large quantity of blood lay above the left shoulder. Body was cold, however the intestines were still warm.
The uterus, fallopian tubes, ovaries, upper portion of the vagina along with two-thirds of the bladder were removed from both the body and the murder site. The incisions avoided the rectum and divided the vagina low enough to avoid damage to the cervix uteri.

Conclusions drawn about the killer:

☛ Some anatomical knowledge
☛ The Killer could not have performed all of the injuries himself in less than 15 minutes.
☛ If the injuries had been done deliberately by a surgeon, it would have taken at least an hour.
☛ Likely the injuries to the throat and abdomen were done with the same instrument, a knife with a thin, narrow blade of at least 6 to 8 inches long. Not a bayonet or a knife used in leather trade. More like a ground-down slaughter man's knife or a small amputating knife.
☛ Murderer strangled or suffocated Chapman to death before mutilations and throat cutting.
☛ The lips, face and hands were livid from asphyxia.

Name: Elizabeth Stride
Age: 44 Years old
Height: 5'2"
Description:
Dark brown hair, light grey eyes, pale complexion, oval face, upper front teeth missing.
Time of Death: 1 October 1888

Post Mortem:
October 1, 1888

Note: The body was stripped by the doctors themselves unlike the last two victims.

A clean incision of about 6 inches from left to right was found on the victim's throat. There were no other cuts or marks to suggest strangulation. There were pressure marks over both shoulders, under the collar bones and in front of the chest caused by the pressure of two hands on the shoulders.

Cause of death was exsanguinated from a partial severance of the left carotid artery and the division of the windpipe. There is a possibility that Stride's throat was cut while she was falling to the ground or when laying on the ground due to the blood spatter patterns.

Conclusions drawn about the killer:

☛ This suggests that the victim was grabbed by the shoulders and pushed to the ground. Murderer was on her right side and had cut her throat from left to right. It would have taken mere seconds to inflict the injury.

Name: Catharine Eddowes
Age: 46 Years old
Height: 5'0"
Description: Dark auburn hair, hazel eyes, "TC" tattoo in blue ink on left forearm. Clothing: Black straw bonnet with green trim and black velvet. Black beads, black cloth jacket with imitation fur around collar and sleeves, green chintz skirt, brown linsey dress bodice and piece of old white apron.
Time of Death: 30 September 1888

Post Mortem:
September 30, 1888

The first victim where the face was mutilated. A cut of a quarter inch through the lower left eyelid, dividing the structures completely through. There was a scratch through the skin on the left upper eyelid near the angle of the nose. The right eyelid was cut through to half an inch. A deep cut over the bridge of the nose starting from the left border of the nasal bone, down to the angle of the jaw on the right side of the cheek. Cut went to the bone, dividing all structures of the cheek except the mucous membranes of the mouth. Tip of the nose was sliced off.

A downward cut from the wings of the nose joined the face, dividing the upper lip and cutting through the gum line. An incision was found on each side of the cheek which peeled up the skin and created a triangular flap. Throat was slit across and the wound was 6 to 7 inches in length. Cut started about 2.5 inches below and behind the left ear and extended across the throat to about 3 inches below the lobe of the right ear.

The sternocleidomastoid muscles of the neck (larger platysma muscles) were divided through the left side, and the larynx was severed below the vocal cords. Cause of death was exsanguinated from the left common carotid artery. Death was immediate and the mutilations were inflicted post mortem.

The front walls of the abdomen were laid open from breast bone to pubis. Incision went upwards. Liver was stabbed by a sharp instrument. Another incision into the liver of 2.5 inches and below this the left lobe of the liver was slit through by a vertical cut. The Abdominal walls were divided into middle line within a quarter inch of the navel. The cut took a horizontal course 2.5 inches toward the right side. It divided around the navel on the left side and made parallel incisions to the former horizontal incision. It then went down the right side of the vagina and the rectum.

A stab on the left of the groin and an incision of 3 inches below this was also present. A cut was made an inch below the crease of the left thigh down the inner side of the thigh, separating the left labium and forming a flap of skin up to the groin. The thigh present with a flap of skin caused by the same type of incision.
Pancreas was cut but not removed. The left kidney was carefully removed and taken by the killer.

The uterus was cut through horizontally and taken away with some of the ligaments while leaving a three quarter inch stump. This suggests that the victim was supine on the ground, on her back.
The instrument was at least a 6 inch blade. It is likely that the mutilations were performed on site where the body was discovered and that the site was not a dump site due to the clotting of the blood at the left of the body and blood spatter patterns.

Conclusions drawn about the killer:

☛ The injuries are seen to be the work of one killer.
☛ Has anatomical knowledge due to the precise removal of the kidney.
☛ The killer is an organized, intelligent male.
☛ He has escalated his mutilations suggesting a primal rage towards women.
☛ The close quarters of the attacks suggest these are of a personal nature.
☛ He is not an ambush killer, he approaches with charisma, poise and head on.

Leo paused briefly, scanning the room of faces in front of him. They always missed this part. The fact that Eddowes and Stride were a double homicide. This was an important piece of information that the students should have picked up on. It was a classic testament to an evolving serial killer who was escalating his kills. It also suggested that Jackie boy had possibly either felt exposed at the first site or was interrupted by someone. Even both and had to abandon his first victim that night leading to the second victim. That meant he needed a replacement hence the double homicide and the primal rage in the second kill.

Leo picked up the second stack of papers he had in front of him. Photocopies of the forensics for the Ripper letters. He started handing them out to the first student in each row of desks. Looking at the woman who'd been dogging him all lecture in the eye as he handed her the stack and watched her pass back the handouts. He smiled as her eyes widened and she realized they were jumping to the letters instead of talking about the last victim just yet. Here it comes, Leo mused.

"Why are we jumping to the letters, isn't there one more victim"

Leo chuckled softly, of course the green eyed beauty in the front row would pipe up. He wasn't surprised, she seemed keen on the subject matter. Almost giddy for it. That was a touch disturbing to Leo in a way. "They" say that you pass by a psychopath at least once in your lifetime without even knowing about it and meet up with plenty of sociopaths in that same lifetime while both knowing and not knowing about it. Leo had seen his share of both while knowing it. He had vowed a long time ago, just barely out of childhood, he would never not know it ever again. If he didn't know any better, he was staring into the emerald green eyes of a covert psychopath who may not know she was one herself.

"Yes, there is a fifth victim. I'm getting to her. The boss letter is important at this point in the lecture because it ties into the profile of Jack the Ripper and gives us a little bit of an inside look at what he was thinking regarding his victims" Leo responded.

"Aren't those a hoax? They deemed them a hoax at the time." She spat back.

"Well, personally. I don't think they were a hoax. I think the investigators were too quick to deem those letters a hoax. The "From Hell" letter alone suggests forensic countermeasures which would suggest an organized, intelligent killer. The box with the partial kidney that came with the letter, although at the time they couldn't and didn't have DNA testing, it could be logically said that, after the physician who examined the partial kidney deemed it a human one, possibly from a woman of 45 years was in fact likely Catherine Eddowes' kidney that was removed from her body prior. So are the letters significantly relevant at this time?"

Leo watched the woman roll his words around in her head. He waited patiently for that all telling sign, the one a person gets when the light bulb goes on and the brain bells go 'ding, ding, ding, ding'. His lop-sided smile flashed as he saw what he was looking for on her face and he nodded with satisfaction. Back to the lecture then.

"So, let's look at the "Boss" letter shall we?" Leo went on, "'The letter itself was mocking the investigators with the fact that they were blaming the killings on a different serial killer, one they had deemed the "Leather Apron". While John Pizer fit some of the profile as a lunatic who had just been released from an asylum he was not Jack the Ripper. He didn't possess the organizational skills or intelligence that required the knowledge of anatomy, where to cut and remove organs and so forth. This likely, as seen in the "Boss" letter, upset Jack the Ripper in the fact that his work was being credited to someone else. He had to tell the world who was really behind the murders. Mocking them was out of anger and frustration. Teasing them that they were too stupid to figure it out, showing them that his superior intellect was no match for them.'

'This shows that Jack the Ripper was a narcissist, an intellect and desired recognition for his work. It also showed that he desired a particular set of control over the investigation. Steering it into his perceived way. He was injecting himself into the investigation by saying "here I am, catch me if you can". He was telling them I know who you are while you don't know who I am. I can get to you anytime I want to.

He was also trying to control the flow of information from the investigation by asking them to "hold back the letter, there's a bit more work to be done first". This also denotes an organized killer who is meticulous and precise. He thinks it through, he plans it. He will follow the investigation, maybe even inject himself into it. He takes pride in his work."

"But, he left the bodies where he killed them. That suggests a disorganized killer." Again the green eyed beauty Leo smiled. She was challenging him head on. He was starting to like this woman despite the creep factor she had.

"Granted, yes a disorganized killer will leave the body at the site they killed the victim at. However, if the killer is already employing forensic countermeasures than suffice it to say he may be leaving his kills out for everyone to see on top of the counter measures. He lured those women, he spoke to them. He killed them with precision and knew how to quickly. Witnesses came forward to say they'd seen these women with some strange man. Can we assume it was Jack the Ripper they saw them with. Yes...and no. We can only assume, all we have is theories."

Again, Leo watched his words roll around in her head. She mulled them over, opened her mouth to say something but then closed it again. This happened a few times and then as suddenly as she challenged him she nodded as if to say okay, go on then.

"Speaking of countermeasures, The Lusk letter also known as the "From Hell " letter is a fine example, if we hypothesize that Jack the Ripper was using forensic countermeasures. The poorly spelled words, the spelling of kidney as Kidne. The taunting nature of the letter. It's quite different from the postcard and the `Boss" letter. This also suggests an organized killer.

The fact that he indicates that he is "down on whores" and will not stop "ripping" until "buckled" suggests that Jack the Ripper is challenging the investigators to catch him while the "catch me if you can mishter" of the "From Hell" letter reiterates that sentiment while being suggestive of a forensic countermeasure. The letters were sent to top investigators and organizations that supported the investigation. Showing them that Jack the Ripper was well aware of them and could easily get to them.

In the letter he indicates that one victim he would "nip the ear" as if she were cattle, possibly cattle like pigs as he also indicates he gave no time for the one victim to "squeal". This is the piece of evidence that may suggest the letters were not a hoax because this letter was received three days prior to Eddowes being discovered murdered and her ear was indeed "nipped" as it were. It suggests the writer of the letter is indeed the killer as that killer would only have that kind of detailed information."

"Moving on, let's talk about the "Saucy Jack" letter." Leo continued. This is where he will find out if these students can really put two and two together.

"Isn't that the letter about the two killed close together?"

Leo was visibly started from his thought. He looked at the woman who had been challenging him all morning with a raised brow. This was a first, he thought. Well then, time to see what this young lady is made of and how this will play out he smiled.

"Yes, it is. Care to elaborate? What was your name?"

"Ivy, and I sure would like to elaborate. The Saucy Jack postcard indicated that there were two victims killed close to one another and that it was a "double event this time". Which of course, refers to the fact that Stride and Eddowes were both killed nearby each other and on the same night as each other. I believe you're going to suggest that the killer was interrupted and may have felt out in the open for the first victim which incited a rage at being interrupted and consequently pushed him to escalate his violence due to rage and frustration and that's why Eddowes is so mutilated while being the first victim with facial mutilations.

Anger, rage, frustration and devolution of a normally organized serial killer into a disorganized serial killer."

"Well, I'll be damned. Couldn't have said it better myself," Leo grunted, "Shall we move on to the last victim then, maybe you should be giving this lecture instead of me Ivy?"

He watched her blush fiercely and stare down at her desk. Leo sighed, he hadn't meant to be that harsh or dismissive. He'd have to apologize after class to Ivy for being a bit of a brute.

ഋ

VICTIM FIVE: MARY JANE KELLY

Name: Mary Jane Kelly
Age: 25 Years old
Height: 5'7"
Description:
Blonde, blue eyes, fair complexion.
Time of Death: 9 November 1888

The Crime Scene:

Mary Kelly was laying on her back in the middle of the bed and was dressed only in a linen undergarment. Head turned to the left cheek, and left arm close to the body with the forearm lying across the abdomen. Right arm rested on the mattress with the elbow bent and fingers clenched. The body was moved from the right side after the victim was killed due to the pillow and sheet at top-right corner being saturated in blood.

Clothes had been burned in the fire, and a fire was made to illuminate the room to work in by the killer and Mary Jane's clothes were found on a chair at the foot of the bed. The throat had been cut from ear to ear down to the spinal column and the face had been hacked beyond recognition. The breasts cut off. Arms had jagged wounds and the legs wide apart. The skin of the abdomen and thighs had been removed. The abdomen emptied of its viscera. The uterus and kidney had been placed with one breast under the head. While the other breast was found by the right foot. The liver placed between the feet.

The intestines by the right side of the body. The spleen by the left side of the body. The skin that had been removed was resting on the table.

Post Mortem:
November 10th, 1888

Cause of death was exsanguinated from the carotid artery. The face had been cut in all directions. Nose, cheeks, eyebrows and ears were partly removed. Lips were blanched and cut by several incisions running down the chin. Neck was cut through the skin, other tissues and down to fifth and sixth vertebrae of the spinal column. The air passage was cut into the lower part of larynx, through the cricoid cartilage. Both breasts removed by rough circular incisions, skin tissues of abdomen from costal arch to pubis removed in three large flaps. The right thigh was cut to the bone, left was stripped of skin, fascia and muscles as far as knee. Left calf had a long gash through the skin and tissues to deep muscle. Went from knee to 5 inches above the ankle. Lower lobe of right lung broken and torn away. Heart was missing, partly digested fish and potatoes found in abdominal cavity with the remains of the stomach sack.

Conclusions drawn about the killer:

☛ Ritualistic behavior. Primal rage? Less knowledgeable of anatomy?
☛ Is this Jack the Ripper or a copycat? Less organized killer.

"Wow, that's the most brutal murder out of the bunch yet" A student from the back row exclaimed loudly. Leo regarded him for a moment before continuing on with his lecture.

"Well, I'm not sure it was Jack the Ripper. The victimology changed drastically. His victimology is women between forty and fifty years old. Dark hair, between five foot and five foot two, light eyes. While the first four meet that description of his preferred victim, Mary Jane isn't twenty five years old, blonde and five foot seven. Yes she has blue eyes, that may be inconsequential however."

"I don't understand, are we missing something?"

"Yes you are. Accounts of a description of a man seen at the time of some of the murders. One account states that a witness saw a man of about five foot seven inches in height, late twenties, dark complexion with a small dark mustache. He was seen with Elizabeth Stride. The description of his clothing was given as wearing a black diagonal cutaway coat, a hard felt hat, white collar and a tie and was carrying a parcel of 18 inches long and 6 to 8 inches wide. A second witness that night describes the man with Stride as five foot five tall, about thirty with a fair complexion, dark hair, a small brown mustache, full face and broad shoulders. Wearing a dark jacket, dark trousers and a black cap with a peak. The third witness who saw Stride with a man described him as five feet seven inches tall, stout and wearing a long dark overcoat.

When they found Stride, or rather a Jewish jeweler did, she was still warm to the touch and the jeweler articulated that he may have interrupted the killer as he thought that maybe the killer had been in the alleyway beside the body and had run off as he went in to alert others in a nearby club. This would support the ideology that the killer was stunted in his work and had to flee prematurely. Getting back to the description, they are similar descriptions however one detail is slightly different and that's the complexion, but we can surmise that witnesses aren't always accurate to a degree.

We can theorize, if we leave out complexion for this purpose that Jack the Ripper's profile falls along these lines," Leo stated, taking a quick breath to finish the rest, "His preferred victimology is a woman of the age ranges between forty and fifty years of age, their height anywhere between five foot and five foot two inches, they have dark hair and light colored eyes," Leo started while watching Ivy in the front row, "he preferred high risk persons, for example prostitutes, addicts, women with drinking behaviors, who were physically smaller and weaker."

"So, people he could pick on basically?" Ivy grunted harshly.

"That would seem to be the case, he was a charm and harm kind of killer. He would charm his way into their little world then harm them as he saw fit." Leo answered back.

"What a charming fucker."

Leo had to stifle laughter, almost slapped his hand to his mouth at the outburst from Ivy. He was sure he was going to lose it any second now. Leo leaned his head back and swallowed his laugh hard and rolled his shoulders, shaking his head with a huge lop-sided, shit eating grin on his face. It seemed to please Ivy that she'd made him smile like that, she grinned back at him with a comical 'tee hee' kind of look on her face.

"On to the actual profile," Leo chuckled, "'lordy, Jack the Ripper? What can we say about him? Well, he was left handed and his preferred method of killing is exsanguination of the victim by slitting the throat and severing the carotid artery.

He's between five foot five and five foot seven, making him taller than his victims, this suggests he's choosing smaller women to over power them. The fact that he has a working knowledge of anatomy and has fairly precise surgical technique suggests he may have been a slaughter man or a medical professional. I do believe he was likely a slaughter man working in one of the slaughterhouses, it would fit the fact he knew the area well and could navigate the boroughs the way he did.

This would also suggest he may actually live in the immediate area and was hunting his own backyard. It means he likely also stalked and watched his victims, getting to know their routines and comings and goings.' 'He was a solitary man but had enough charisma to lure the women in and get them to follow him or let him in, that's why we call him a charm and harm killer which is much like modern day killers like the Ted Bundys, Paul Bernardos and Karla Holmolkas of our world. Some of his behavior, the blood, ritualistic tendencies and such show the possibility that he may have had a domineering, narcissistic mother or female head of house. This also explains the extreme mutilations of female genitalia and sex organs. It may represent an ingrained, intense hatred of all that represents women. Put that all together and what do we have for a profile? We have a man in his late twenties to early thirties with a moderate to high level intelligence, who has charisma but not enough to be noticed by witnesses which makes him a charm and harm killer. He likely lives in the area as he knows it well enough to get around undetected and escape possible detection when interrupted by someone during a kill.

He is bold, wants recognition and will taunt the investigators while injecting himself into the investigation in order to control or dictate said investigation and investigators. He is intelligent enough to employ forensic countermeasures. While composed for the most part and an organized serial killer who plans his kills he can be triggered into disorganized behavior, as is the case with Catherine Eddowes after being interrupted for Elizabeth Stride. This shows a certain amount of instability, and emotional deterioration. As for Mary Jane Kelly, she doesn't fit the victimology at twenty five and five foot seven inches with blonde hair and blue eyes. The manner in which she was mutilated shows that the killer may have been inexperienced, lacking the knowledge of the previous four murders for anatomy. This murder was ritualistic while the other four were not.

The organ placements and the heart missing indicates that the killer for Mary Jane Kelly was delusional, unhinged and a disorganized killer perhaps with his first kill and trying to evade forensics with countermeasures and copycat behavior. In light of that last comment, it could be said that Jack the Ripper may have become unhinged or was using forensic countermeasures to continue to control and thwart or throw off the investigators.'

'It is possible that Mary Jane Kelly was a Ripper victim and that Jack the Ripper may have even evolved and escalated and that the previous, in his eyes, lesser women were practice killings. Perhaps the women were quite possibly a substitute for his true target. Miss Mary Jane Kelly."

The class gasped in unison. Even Ivy in the front row was visibly stunned by Leo's conclusion to his lecture. He grinned and nodded. Got them every time. He didn't necessarily ascribe to his lecture theory in full but that was the nature of theory wasn't it? As he dismissed the class, Leo started gathering up his papers and lecture notes when her hand lightly touched his. His jaw tightened as he looked up into her green eyes. She was smirking as she stared at him.

"Is Leo short for Leonard?" She quizzed him playfully.

"Most would think so and would be right, but no. Not in my case," he shot back tightly, "Just Leo."

"That theory of yours is interesting, it's the first time I've ever come across it before."

Leo looked beyond Ivy's shoulder line, watching the rest of the class. They were in fevered discussions all over the room. Some arguing that the lecture theory was a load of crock, others arguing that just maybe the theory was exactly why the case had never been solved.

It's exactly what Leo had wanted for the students. To always question and nothing was as it seemed at any given time. Leo looked back at Ivy, raising a brow. She was outright grinning at him, looking him up and down as she did. Leo shivered; this woman really unsettled him.

"Have you ever heard of the asylum case, you know the one with the mutilated male victim in the middle of butt fuck no where forest?"

Leo hid a gasp of his own but the startled look on his face he couldn't hide. He looked down at his lecture notes, shuffling them over again. That was the one case in his younger days that had gotten away on him. The assailant was still at large, most of the case details had never been seen by the public and it was now a cold case. It was his fault that the case was in the cold case pile right now. He'd fucked up, missed details way too late. Evidence had been trampled and he had nearly lost his job over it.

It was a black mark on his personnel file that he absolutely couldn't stand being there.

"How do you know?"

She was gone, Leo cocked his head to one side feeling like he had lost his damn mind. Thinking, maybe he had been talking to himself all this time. He knew she had been there, he could still smell the soft, sweetness of her perfume lingering in the air in front of him. He felt those green eyes boring holes in his own even after she was gone. They were haunting him already. Leo packed the last of his lecture notes and stalled a few moments more. Maybe to avoid possibly running into that strange woman in the hallway but he forced himself to convince his mind it was to see if any of the students decided to ask him more questions. Funny how we convince ourselves out of our fears and feelings isn't it Leo mused.

Slipping his hand into his own pocket he grunted out of surprise. There was a folded up piece of paper in his pocket that wasn't there before. Looking down at it, Leo observed a loose, easy going script like handwriting. A woman's. The only word on the paper was "Lenore". He crumpled the piece of paper angrily and tossed it away from himself. Why, why would she? How could she know? Who the hell is this woman?

ଓ

Just as Leo was packing the last lecture notes into his bag another agent came rushing into the room. Leo raised a brow and looked at Agent Smith with a leeriness. The agent looked winded and was sweaty as if he'd done a long mile a few times around a few blocks.

"What can I do you for Agent Smith?"

"It's happening again Agent Desbrates."

"What is happening again?"

"Killings like the one from the asylum case. It's happening again and they want you in the office asap Agent Desbrates. You're the one who knows the case better than anyone else does. They want you."

"They took me off that case and barred me from it years ago." Leo tried to hide his excitement. He couldn't contain himself and the beat of his heart in his ears and throat was nearly strangling him.

"Just was told to come get you, will you please come now."

"Alright, cool your jets Agent Smith. Let's go." Leo grinned widely. He had a second chance. He didn't think he'd ever get a second chance but here it was. He could clear his black mark from his file and catch the killer.

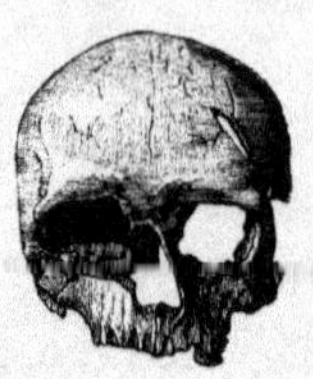

SYMPATHY FOR THE DEVIL. WHEN STONES ROLL DOWNHILL

Troy remembered her. Remembered what she had done in front of him too and how she had left him with that vile bitch of a sister of hers. He'd been told his mother had been schizophrenic. He remembered how she had "heard the voices" that told her to do things. Grotesque things. Things that no little boy should ever witness his mother doing. They would tell her to cut and dig out balls of flesh from her own body. Told her it was her punishment for being a bad little girl. Told her to do things to him. Things that he couldn't even repeat in his mind let alone out loud.

Things he would take to his grave. Things that made Queen Jocasta look like a saint. Just when Troy had thought it couldn't get any worse his mother had spiraled even further with her schizophrenic symptoms. She had started to see things he couldn't see. Slapping at them like little flies buzzing about her head. She hadn't showered in weeks, she was rank, dirty and her hair was a crow's nest of knots in every direction about her head like some sick version of Christ's crown of thorns.

He'd found her rocking back and forth in the corner of her room that night. Whispering and picking at her skin. Blood on her fingers tips, lips and on the floor and walls around her. Rocking and picking, rocking and picking. He had tried to make her stop, he hated when she did that whispering thing, looking all around like something was tormenting her. Her eyes had gotten this glazed look suddenly then they had rolled back for a few minutes. Troy had been sure she was about to take a fit or something when her eyes focused on him intensely.

"Boy. They say you are my most evil invention."

"Who is they mama?"

"All knowing They. They know everything, they tell me things don't you know. Deep, dark dangerous things. Things that make me bleed because I'm a bad little girl don't you know?"

Troy hadn't been sure what his mother was talking about, he didn't even know how to turn on the stove let alone figure out adults. He had tried again to make his mother stop rocking and picking but she had pulled away from him and spun around, putting her back to him. When she turned back around she had this strange huge grin on her face. It stretched across her skin tightly, Troy never thought a person's skin could stretch that far like that. It had made mommy look like some terrible, under the bed monster that gave little boys and girls horrible nightmares.

His mother had leaned forward, still grinning wildly when she had taken the switchblade from under her dress folds and carved her mouth wider, splitting both cheeks into double flaps on either side of the horrific grin on her face. Troy had screamed and pissed himself but couldn't run, he'd been frozen in place with sheer utter terror. He remembered trying to tell her no when she brought the switchblade to her left eye and plucked it from its socket, the eye dangling from its mooring like a tether ball on its rope from the pole. A swift flick of her wrist and her right eye ended up joining the left on the other side of her face.

That's when she had turned the blade downward and slit her own throat from ear to ear. Blood gushing everywhere, Troy stepping back as his mother had flopped onto the floor gasping like a fish out of water, that insane grin never leaving her mouth.

The neighbors had heard Troy screaming which prompted them to come rushing over to the house Hope and her boy, Troy lived at. It was a dilapidated little two bedroom, one bath. It had been the family bungalow from when Hope and her sister, Grace had been children. The Islows had been neighbors since the girls parents had built the little one floor house.

When Mrs. Islow ran into the room she couldn't help but scream in horror and snatch up Troy. He had been babbling uncontrollably with snot and tears streaming down his face. Sat in his mother's pooling blood with both her eyes staring up at him from the ends of their nerves on each side of her face. A grin had been stretched across her face that would put Batman's Joker to full shame if he'd seen it.

ଓ

The social workers, police and detectives had a terrible time trying to locate the boy's aunt. Gracie Haimon was not a woman who liked to be found. She hated just about everything in life, including her family of origin. Her father had been a mean drunk asshole and her sister had been the "golden child" for her mother. Her mother had been a narcissistic mound of stupid. Gracie certainly didn't want the brat child her sister Hope had left behind, the out of wed-lock brat. Why did it have to be her issue? She didn't spread her stupid ass legs and make a useless thing. The social worker was sitting across from Gracie expectantly, not so patiently though. Gracie sighed.

"Repeat that, I'm sorry dear, didn't quite hear your question."

"Are you willing to take your nephew Troy, Miss Haimon? We give a monthly stipend to help pay for the child's needs. It's quite a generous stipend as well."

A stipend! Money to take care of a brat? Well then, Gracie smiled sweetly. He might be worth the trouble after all. She could go for free money. He might actually prove to be more useful than his bitch mother had ever been.

"Of course, family does for family don't they." Gracie poured the sweetness into her words thick and heavy.

☙

The first few months were heaven compared to what Troy had grown up with. He had suspected, when he was old enough to suspect, that his Auntie Gracie had been playing prim and proper because of the social workers coming around and checking up on him and his aunt. Making sure their stipend was going to him as the child and that he was in a safe place. Auntie Gracie had fooled them all. Played the loving and doting Auntie with her "oh dear child, you poor sweet thing, you've gone through hell haven't you," in front of the social workers. It was a whole different story when their backs were turned though hadn't it been.

When the workers weren't around she worked him like a dog. Scrubbing the toilet, floors, walls. If he didn't do it right, which was about all the time, she would make him strip naked and kneel in raw rice in front of the crucifix on her wall in the living room. She would yell "pray you horrid little beast child, pray you don't gouge your eyes out too". She would sometimes make him get a branch from her back gardens and she'd whip him with it, screaming about him being a sinner just like his mother.

"You sinner, you evil little vile thing. Just like your mother. Lazy and stupid."

Out in public was like the social workers. She was sweet as pie when people were looking. Couldn't risk that stipend could she. Couldn't risk her little paycheck. She'd make sure the bruises and cigarette burns were easy to hide. She'd make him recite the things he would have to say to the social workers. While he did, tell them what Auntie Gracie wanted them to hear, she'd make sure he saw her behind them giving him that look that she was so good at giving. The kind that makes little children shrivel up and screech running to their mommies and daddies beds because the monster under the bed tried to eat them. The day she had finally pushed him to the snapping point was the day she had been in a particularly foul mood.

He'd had a friend over and they were hanging out in his room after school. He had always teased this girl, he liked her. She had pretty blue-gray eyes and dark, wavy black hair. It wasn't quite curls but almost. She was petite but she was also wiry and built like a tank at the same time. It was like she was a girl with a penis sometimes. Tough but soft at times too. He had found her attractive in an odd sort of way. Troy was teasing her softly when Auntie Gracie had come barreling into the room screaming about bad boys and girls who diddle each other and how God would punish them for their indecencies. She had humiliated Troy in front of the girl.

The girl had left, head down and crying while Auntie Gracie had chased her out of the house with her religious sermon, ranting at his friend like some fucked up televangelist proselytizing about brim fire and the circles of hell. Troy had felt the rage boil up from the core of his being. It had rolled in at a quick clip at the center of his chest. It had felt the same as when you thought you were going to puke but way better than that. He had been shaking as he walked on numb wobbly legs to the kitchen that day. Eyes searching around for something, he had just enough time to think "what was I looking for?" When his eyes had settled on the Henckels knife on the counter. She used his money for that fancy little Henckels knife set. Along with a lot of other expensive splurges over the years.

How fitting Troy had thought to himself when he plucked it from the counter. She had been in the living room, smirking at her handy work, watching through the curtains as his friend flew down the driveway on her radial bike and down the street they all lived on. The crunch of her spine under the knife as it broke had surprised Troy quite a bit. It was a sound he hadn't expected, just as much as the screaming that followed wasn't what he had expected either. It was guttural and choked at the same time. He never thought a human being could ever have made a sound like that.

It had stirred something in Troy. At first he had been disturbed by what it was, it confused him at the time. He had felt, aroused by her screams of pain. It had given him the hardest erection he'd ever had. It was like he was a kid discovering how to tickle the pole all over again. Troy had sunk to the carpet with his aunt putting a hand over her mouth to quiet her in case anyone should end up hearing it. He had known that they wouldn't think twice of her screaming a little bit because she screamed at him all the time. The neighbors would just chalk it up to another Graceful Gracie screaming fit.

When he realized she couldn't move he ended up grinning down at her. That's when he had known she knew she was in more than a bit of trouble. Troy had felt giddy, his skin tingled as his aunt whimpered and pleaded with him to help her. She had gone through the stages of grief, though Troy hadn't been sure what she had to grieve, certainly not her stinking life being that it was worthless. First she had skipped denial, wasn't any way you could deny the blade in her spine. Went straight to bargaining or was that begging. He preferred begging. Then she had jumped backward to anger, he had cured her of that pretty quick by wrapping his hands around her throat and squeezing just short of making her pass out, he had wanted her to feel every bit of it. To make her pay.

When she finally skipped depression and jumped to acceptance Troy had moaned softly and looked away for a moment. He had been ashamed at first that it had made him climax to watch her just accept her fate like that. That shame had made him feel the boiling rage again and he had carved her like a Thanksgiving turkey. Stabbing and slashing and ripping at her fat ass flesh like a frenzied animal. Growling and spitting curses and names at her while the light died out from her eyes. How she dared to make him feel shame for what was her fault. This time, it had been her fault. Not his.

The next day, he'd come to, on the floor next to his aunt's dead and cold body. He'd panicked at first. Running around in circles babbling about what was he supposed to do, how was he supposed to clean this mess up. He had to give his head a shake, take a deep breath and think. He'd finally come up with an idea. Chop her up in the tub, he'd thought. Then he could get rid of the pieces a little at a time. That would work he'd whispered, and it did. He ended up spending the next few weeks toting around pieces of his auntie Gracie and dumping her around the neighborhood.

☙

"What'cha got in the bag Troy?"

Troy grit his teeth, she was bouncing around him like some little wiry terrier dog. He was still reeling from Auntie Gracie's demise by Henkels too. Dumpster Kid could be an annoying brat but she was a pretty annoying brat. Blue-grey eyes, almost curly black hair. Wiry, built but femme as well. Troy found himself eying Dumpster Kid up and down. She was standing there, head cocked to one side with a lop-sided shit eating grin on her face and a raised brow. He had to laugh, she was always a riot. Little brat.

"Just stuff. Never mind that. Want to hang out at my place tonight?"

"Your Aunt gonna be there? I really don't like her, no offence."

"No she went away on a trip to go help a relative. No offence taken, don't like her either."

"Okay then, want me to bring over the newest comics I got over the weekend?"

Troy grinned. The girl with the proverbial penis. He liked the fact that he could jock around with Dumpster Kid and still look at a pretty girl and pretty girl boobs too. She was different from Ivy, she was more athletic than Ivy was. Where Ivy was feminine and dainty, Dumpster Kid was rough and tumble. It was a stark contrast, Troy had heard words from the adults around them about girls like her. Dyke, Butch, Tom Boy.

The kids could be cruel but some of the adults around them were even more so than the kids. Always whispering around them, covert comments and stares. She didn't seem to notice, Troy thought, or maybe she did but didn't say anything about it.

"Yeah, sure. Bring them over. We'll have the house to ourselves."

"Hey!" It made them both jump. It was Ivy. Strutting along down the street toward them, wheeling her bike beside her with a flat tire on the front. Troy smirked, it was the third time this month she'd had a flat. Girl had no luck with bike tires. Troy's smile faded as he watched Dumpster Kid look from the flat tire to the ground with a weird look. His brow raised as it occurred to him the look on her face was jealousy, pure unadulterated jealousy.

Well, it looks like we know who's responsible for all the flat tires don't we? Troy would have to bring that up later to her.

"Hey, come here you two," Ivy waved them both closer, dropping her bike to the ground, "let's take a picture, the three of us. The summer of the Lost Kids Club. What'dya say?"

All three of them scooted in close. Ivy turned the Polaroid camera to themselves and screamed "say cheesie doodles' ' and snapped a shot. She stood there looking back at both Troy and Dumpster Kid with a big wide grin while waving the Polaroid around in the air.

"This one will be great for the album."

"Wait, you keep an album of all of us?" Dumpster Kid grunted at her.

"Not just you dumb dumbs, various things." Ivy snarked back.

Troy just shook his head, picked up Ivy's bike and started rolling it back to his driveway. He'd fix it again for Ivy and have to have a serious chat with Dumpster Kid about knocking it off with the flat tires.

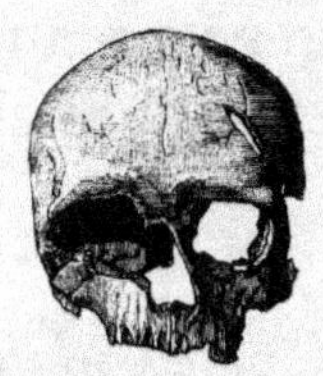

THE DEVIL WITH HIS DOLL

The hallway is dark and dingy. There is very little light. The buzz of the run down overhead halogen echoing slightly off the walls. Tapping sounds float out from the door at the end of the hall. 'tap tap tap', a pause and again, 'tap tap tap'. A mutter of soft words as if under the breath. Someone talking to someone else. It gets a little heated but only one side of the conversation can be heard.

"You should have listened to me, I told you so," the voice mutters, "they never listen."

Moving down the hallway, the door looms foreboding, a heavy oak door with years of wear and tear. Streaks of paint from different decades etch across the four-panels. Chipped and peeling, it shows the different stages of color schemes used over the years, almost reminiscent of a broken jaw breaker with its multicolored stripes. The door is heavy, pushing it open reveals a harsh laboratory light that spills into the dank recesses of the hallway.

He can be seen sitting there tapping a scalpel, smirking at the body in front of him on a shiny stainless-steel table. The tapping of the scalpel on the cadaver table accentuates every rock back and forth of his head as he plans his next cut, thinking to himself that it must be perfect, this type of art takes not only precision but talent. Both of which he has, after all, he is an artist don't you know. The smell in the room is almost sickly sweet. Formaldehyde and candy mixed together. The chemicals searing the nostrils and throat while the sweet candy smell could choke a bull elephant.

It's like death meets bittersweet and that can be dangerously soothing at first but nefariously deceiving underneath.

☙

It's so cold here, I can't believe how cold and my toe itches, if only I knew how to reach it but alas I can't seem to reach it. Why did they put me in this outfit? What is wrong with them? Don't they know I don't like plaid?

☙

"She would kill me if she knew I'd put her in this outfit," he says straightening out and smoothing the plaid slacks.

☙

All these thoughts swirling in my head, but it's pointless isn't it? All I can feel is the cold. I don't know why I am obsessed with my toe, or why I have this insane sense of regret. I feel like I should be doing something right now, but I don't know exactly what. I feel myself slipping into unconsciousness, and yet I am awake and alive.

What is this sensation? I can feel my skin and it feels so different, its wet, and cold, and smells funny. Yet, I feel peaceful and somehow completely aware of myself, like I am floating in a deep and dark abyss and yet I can't quite shake the feeling that I should be slightly more concerned about this feeling of cold, this smell of rot and the fact that this toe will not stop itching. I loved him.

It was not just the kind of love you feel when you're a young stupid girl who is writing 'I HEART XX' on your binder at school. I loved him so much I would fucking do anything for him, and I did, didn't I. But, this is not where it began. It was innocent at first. I loved him from the moment we met. It was a day like any other, me grabbing my soy latte at Starbucks, and that's when I met him. I turned around from the counter and there he was, directly behind me.

He was tall and slender, with red hair and these deep blue eyes. He was rocking a pair of denim blue jeans and a simple black t-shirt, I don't remember his shoes, it was his eyes I remember the most. He smiled at me, and I smiled back and for some reason as I stood there at the cream counter adding in two packets of sugar and some half and half, he approached me. I felt like my heart was beating out of my chest. I wanted him to talk to me, I wanted him to ask me my name, I felt dizzy.

ᏍᏍ

"Hello there" he said, his voice as smooth as silk

"Hi", I squeaked, trying my best to avoid him making me blush

"I don't usually do this, but um, would you like to have a coffee with me?" He asked, his voice was now a deep resonating sound that seem to feel like I was drawn into him, and yes I wanted that coffee, perhaps even more than just that, but now I am certain, that thinking just about him in that way, was making me blush.

"OK" was all I could muster

"What's your name?" He asked, ushering me toward a nearby table.

"Ivy" I replied

"Nice to meet you Ivy" he smiled back at me.

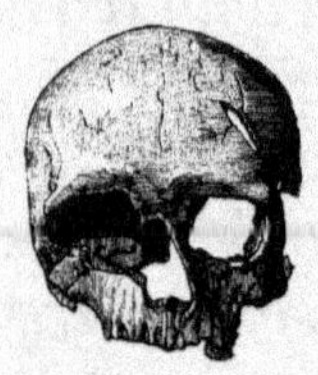

MEETING HIS DARK FLOWER

The woman was something he had never set eyes on before in his life. This beautiful creature had a smile that could charm the devil himself he thought. I must have her. Troy moved a little closer to her in the line of the Starbucks. Time to turn up the charm. Troy smiled his lopsided grin, the one that puts a twinkle in his eye. Women generally couldn't resist that lopsided grin of his, but this woman wasn't paying attention. Damn.

He looked at her again, watching her inspect a sugar packet closely then reject it and put it back down. He watched this cycle of picking the packet up, inspecting it and rejecting it until she finally found one she wanted. He cocked his head to one side and raised a brow. Glancing down, he gently reached out and flicked one of the bins of packets at the bottom, sending a cascade of sugar packets across the floor and their feet. When he looked up, the eyes that stared incredulously back at him took his breath away.

"Why did you do that?" She asked in a huff.

"I, uhm, sorry?" Troy stammered, "I was uhm, reaching for it. I guess I knocked everything over huh"

The woman shook her head and smiled softly, Troy smirked and shrugged his shoulders at her as if to say 'heh, yeah ops'. She giggled at him and smiled again.

"Uh, I don't usually do this but would you? Well, like to go for coffee sometime? I'm Troy, " he said offering his hand to this little pixie of a woman.

"I'm Ivy," the woman squeaked, "sure, why not."

I can't describe how that smile felt, I should have detected then what I know now, but how can you. How can you know and that was it. It was the beginning of a relationship that would transform me. I can't describe how much our love was like a run-away freight train.

It was a quick transition from dating to living together to full on committed living together. It seemed like the days just bled one to the next with little break between. If only I could itch that toe though. That hasn't changed, the itch is still there, but now it's burning, more intense and I can't tell you how much it's still so cold. I wonder if I am dreaming, if this is all just not happening. I think back to the sheets. The sheets of our bed are so hot from his body, enveloping me like warm water, he smells good, he tastes good. His smile draws me in, sometimes bearing his beautiful teeth in a playful way to say, I might devour you my love and how much I want that to be true. Devour me, consume me, I am yours. The flashes of his face seem to almost fade for me now, but I am recalling something on my hands, what is it, I cannot see it. Help me, it's so cold, so cold and that toe just keeps itching.

How they met was not purely by chance at all, Troy scoped out his hunting grounds, and there were several hunting grounds, for ripe pickings on a regular basis. This was just another doe in his headlights, albeit a very rare and beautiful doe, ready to be picked off by him. He had seen her back in the mall at the natural foods store obviously rifling through the discount bin and followed her to the Starbucks. Why did they always seem so oblivious to their surroundings – foolish little creatures. Didn't they know there were predators lurking or were they so satiated by their false sense of securities that they no longer had instincts left for danger.

Her beauty was something to behold.

This dark haired and green-eyed doe. Her eyes were what got to him the most. A deep emerald green that he could lose himself in. She was the first woman who had taken him by surprise at what she stirred in him. He had not expected her, she blind sided him completely.

He might even hazard to say that she stirred some version of love in him. Not love that any normal sane person might describe but rather his own twisted and sinister version. There was a lot he hadn't expected with her. She had been easy enough to target but, in a way, without them both knowing it, she had targeted him as well. She had this, seemingly soft and gentle nature but there was something darker roiling just beneath that.

Something, familiarly sinister even. Like sweet cherry candies. The ones that if you eat too many of them it makes your gut roll but eat just the right amount and its heaven in your mouth – but there is always that fine line with both those candies and Ivy. Troy stared at himself in the mirror then looked past himself at the bed where she was laying on her belly under the silk white sheets. The curve of her shoulder just poking out of the sheet while the silhouette of her hips and ass tried to entice him back into bed. Troy felt the heat of himself start to respond with a twinge and then an ache, he had work to do though. No time for a second round of her sweetness, it would have to wait.

☙

The sheets were wet and cold, and the smell of cologne and sweat dripped from our bodies as they twisted in the sheets. The feeling that I was falling and floating all hit me like a ton of bricks. I wanted to consume him, devour him. I was giving myself to him over and over. There was something else in the room, but what it was now, I don't know. What is that? What is that in my hand? What is that feeling, I am rocking and swaying and so cold, so cold. I hear him call me, "Ivy. Ivy, I love you. Come to me darling, come." I feel him around me, and in that hour of my longing and needing that can't be satisfied.

How did it come to this, these sheets, the cold, my toe and yet I keep feeling myself back in his arms, he holds me and cradles me against his chest. His heart beats so rapidly, and he smells so good, but something isn't right is it, something is wrong, so wrong.

I just don't know.

Around the apartment the mood was still, it was calm and quiet, the iPod pumping out the same old song, what was it about that song? He always listened to it, especially when he came back from his trips away. I never knew where he went, and honestly never asked. I had surrendered myself to Troy fully, I would never disobey him nor flout him in any way, I belonged to him, heart and soul.

The apartment was never the same without him there, it was like a dead zone, empty and sad. I would remain ready for him coming home, never going into the room he told me to avoid, never asking questions, maybe I should have, maybe I will. Then there is his eyes, his eyes are deep pools that make me lose whatever inhibitions I had, if I ever had any. Maybe the true Ivy is the one that lives for him, that holds him and is with him, but there it is, that toe again, why can't I scratch it? What's wrong with me? I simply can't hold on to the visions of him, I am falling and it is dark here.

ଓ

Troy smiled softly and picked up the brush with a raised brow. Brushing through his curly blonde hair while contemplating his work at hand. Staring into his own piercing deep blue eyes and running his tongue across his upper teeth, Troy smirked playfully. There were a few new cuts to his art he needed to make this afternoon. He had found the perfect silky fabric for the new piece of art as well, finally, found the right one. Putting the brush down, Troy slowly pulled out a pair of briefs from the drawer, only pausing when Ivy stirred a little then settled. He threw on his briefs and went searching for his pants and button up shirt that Ivy had so unceremoniously torn off his body last night in her moment of heat. Time to get to work, Troy grinned as he kissed Ivy on the temple softly.

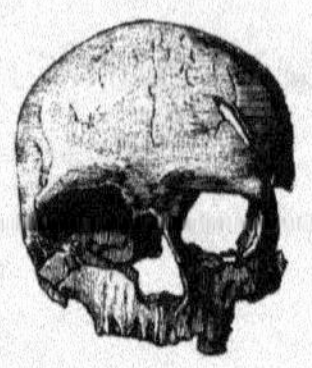

THE DOE BECOMES THE DOLL

I woke up with the bed empty and cold, but his shirt had been left there just waiting to hold me and tell me all the truth I wanted to hear. The apartment smelled like lemon, almost antiseptic. There was a new present for me laid out on the dresser. A silver locket lay there ready to be placed on my neck. I put it on and smiled. My body was still shivering from the night before, riding the sheets like waves was hard on me, but I simply composed myself, walked to the fridge, grabbed an apple and bit into its flesh.

I took myself in the shower to clean off from last night. The shower was odd this morning, a lot of towels again, Troy must have cut himself shaving again. I get into the stall, feel the steam, but that's all. I don't remember now what I was doing, or what soap I was using. I do remember stepping out of the shower, looking in the mirror. I was not Ivy anymore. I was his Ivy. A different Ivy. As simple as washing my hands, I became another Ivy again. Stripping the form of me off like tearing paper, and donning the new Ivy.

Stitch this here, primp that there, hide this, cover that, but something of me always remains. I like the dead eye dolls containing the hidden things, they look at you, the mimic expression, but they are not alive, and nor am I. The hum of the car tires on the highway was always soothing to Troy's frayed nerves. He was antsy, fidgeting badly with the knob of the shifter. Caressing it back and forth with the palm of his hand. Wishing he could slam the accelerator a little heavier but if he got stopped by a cop that would be very bad right now. Patience Troy, he told himself.

The song blaring out of the car speakers was his favorite hunting song. Though he had bagged his little prize replacement doe for this piece of artwork, she was in the trunk right now, he had to move his prize. He hated having to move his work. It disrupted his artistic creativity. Sometimes he even lost his mojo and had to start all over, but Ivy had been lingering too long at that door.

The look of curiosity was too much for him to bare leaving his work where she might find it. Just in case she might get too curious. He wasn't ready for her artwork yet, not nearly close to ready to start that one.

He needed more time to finish this one first and prep for hers. The music blaring in the background, almost a scream at the level Troy had it playing at.

...Does she know that we bleed the same...

He caressed the knob of the shifter again before shifting into fourth gear, the burr of the engine responding to his demands easily enough. He would be there soon, hopefully he would have enough daylight to make it to his work space with his precious doe without ruining what he had already started. The forest grew denser as the car careened further off the beaten path. There was no one to hear the muffled moans from Troy's car, no one to hear the thump against the hood of the trunk. She was a tiny little thing, five foot something and maybe a hundred pounds soaking wet.

She was tied up, trussed like a Sunday turkey dinner and naked as the day she was born. Her hair was shorn short, bald patches here and there on her scalp where the scissors cut a little too close. She moaned, tried to roll to her side but instead set her crushed wrist to screaming hot white pain up her arm again. Kristin couldn't understand why this was happening to her.

Why had he done this to her? What did she do to him? Her mind raced through every possible scenario that could happen from here out, what were his plans? She did know one thing for sure, his plans included her dying. She knew this like she knew the feel of her own heart beat against her chest. Troy slammed the car to a stop at the beginnings of a dirt road wedged between two crops of pine and birch trees.

He nearly missed, he always nearly missed it, so much so that it became a habit now. Damn autopilot.

Thump. Thump. Thump.

"Knock it off bitch" Troy growled loudly through clenched teeth, thumping his fist on the steering wheel. There was a whimper and then silence.

Troy shook his head and grunted. This little doe was feisty, a fighter. It sometimes gave Troy a wicked hard on when they fought him, he liked the feisty ones but today was not one of those days. They may be out in the middle of butt fuck no where bush but there were still prying eyes on occasion even out here. He had to move quickly or else risk losing his beloved prized doe.

Bombing down the dirt road at breakneck speed Troy yanked the steering wheel with a hard left, nearly careening into a crop of three birch trees. He got so close to them he could see the thin papery bark peeling off the trunks in his side mirror. God damn Troy. Patience man, patience, he cussed himself out. As he was about to holler back at the bitch whimpering in his trunk again his eyes fell on the bunker door at the end of the dirt path. If you didn't know what you were looking for you would miss that as easily as you can miss the dirt road itself.

It was tucked away into a densely packed thicket of bushes, trees and rocks. Absentmindedly, Troy fingered the key on his key ring. The key to the very bunker tucked away in the middle of the bush. He had found it quite by accident, had to have the lock retooled by a locksmith after purchasing the land it was on. It was left overs from a long-ago fevered mind that thought the world was coming to an end in the seventies. Old coot's family let the acres go cheap too, a last remnant of a long-passed family member that they didn't want to remember.

Troy rolled his car to a hard-jerking stop, hopefully the bitch back there would finally shut up long enough for him to think straight. He slammed it in the park and cranked the, music down to a whisper.

...did she run away, did she run away ...I don't know...

Troy slid out of the driver's seat while pulling the keys out of the ignition. Trotting to the back of the vehicle he tapped along the side of it and over the hood of the trunk with a wide lopsided grin. He chuckled when the prized doe more than whimpered at his impending approach.

"Doesn't that sound like inevitability dear precious doe," Troy purred through the trunk of the car, tapping softly with every syllable, "you will make a fine *pièce de résistance* my sweet darling doe."

He sighed softly as he jammed the key into the lock of the trunk, turning it. The trunk flew open wildly startling Troy backwards. Oh, that fucking bitch. Troy looked up in time to see a pair of feet come flying at him and he barely had time to side step it. Kristin clipped him in the shoulder sending him twisting around and sprawling across the leaves and dirt.

"For fucks sake" Troy cursed loudly as he rolled away from another attempt at Kristin trying to kick him. Seems she somehow slipped her ropes around her ankles and was now attempting to escape him he thought as he rolled away, barely missing getting kicked in the side of the head, and grabbed her ankle then yanked upward hard. The thud of her landing on her ass squarely in the leaves made Troy bare his teeth in a primal growl of satisfaction. She has brass ones to pull this shit, now look at her. She's all dirty and full of mud and leaves. It's ruined, just ruined.

Troy glared at her as he came to his knees, the stupid bitch ruined it. Just completely ruined it and now he was going to have to start all over again. Why did she have to be such an ungrateful goddamn bitch. Didn't she know she was destined to be a beautiful piece of art, forever etched into time immortal. Some people just couldn't take a gift without ruining it for everyone else. Troy's face reddened with pure rage and the scream that poured from the core of his being and out his mouth was more animal than man.

It was over so fast Troy himself didn't have time to realize it at first either. The shick of the switchblade as he produced it from his pocket and the sweet sickly rip of skin, followed by the coppery smell and slippery feel of Kristin's blood splashing his face and neck. His hands had done his thinking for him and he had slit her throat in a blind rage. Now he would have to find another replacement doe for the artwork. How disappointing.

...come back home...

ꟹ

Kristin was tiny enough for Troy to carry over one shoulder. His clothes were soaked in her now coagulating blood. It had been surprising how long it had taken her to bleed out and die. She truly had been quite the fighter. Troy had lain next to her on the bed of leaves and stared into her eyes while she choked to death on her own blood and she had stared him right back in the eyes with this glare as she died, feisty little precious doe, a shame to waste such a beauty. Patting her bare ass with his hand Troy nodded and produced the key to the bunker door, unlocking it.

Walking down the dingy hallway of the bunker in the dark he started whistling softly to ease the eerie feeling he had slithering up his spine. The hallway of the bunker kind of creeped even Troy out. The echo of his footfalls sounded like little lost souls howling out of the dark shadowy corners. Sometimes he swore you could almost hear them whispering from the darkness.

Why? What did we do to you Troy?

Help me, he won't let me go.

You are going to die like we did Troy, you'll see, you will.

Troy shivered as he came to the four-panel door at the end of the hallway. As he opened the door he flicked the light switch bringing to life a glaring halogen light that hummed miserably. The shine of the cadaver table in the middle of the room made Troy squint a bit. He flipped Kristin off his shoulder and coldly slapped her body down on the table.

Staring at her open eyes and face Troy smiled softly and cocked his head to one side, picking up his scalpel from the medical side table he reached for the woman on his table. Just a little slit there and a big cut here,maybe I can salvage this into something else. He would still need a new doe for the current piece he was working on though.

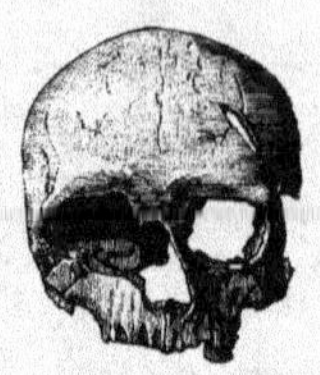

DINNER WITH THE DEVIL

It was on our anniversary that I asked Troy to share more about himself. It seems kind of dumb in retrospect that I never asked him about his work. The photography in the apartment of bondage and death was always curious to me. But, I figured he was just an eclectic artist, like many of my boyfriends, he liked the same macabre things I did. We always enjoyed the darkness together, and Troy was very much that side of me. The dark Ivy, the Ivy that liked to play in the shadows. She had surprised him with her question out of nowhere. They were at the restaurant for their anniversary. One year already.

My does time fly, Troy mused to himself as he twirled the dessert spoon in his fingers. He was lost in thought and the spoon when she asked him to share more about himself. His eyes had flicked from the spoon to her while pursing his lips. Caution Troy, his mind screamed.

The last time you shared anything with someone it ended badly, Troy frowned, started for a punishment with a spoon to the back of the hand because of being mouthy and ended with broken fingers and a whole lot of blood to clean up that night.

He shook it off though, this was Ivy. His beloved Ivy, his dark and twisted flower that wrapped and enveloped him with her deadly vines of desire, choking him just enough to elicit the most wicked of heat in him but not enough to squash the life out of him either. She was a fine balance of pain and pleasure, his dark little Ivy. Then again, he had been following her when her curiosity peaked, and she started snooping around the locked door.

One night he followed her to the police station. She had cried all the way there in the rain, looking over her shoulder like some sneaky child trying to get away with the whole cookie jar let alone one of the cookies. He had watched as she left a letter in the outdoor mailbox of the precinct then slink quickly off down the alleyway beside the building. Troy then trotted up to the mailbox and dug for the envelope. When he had pulled it out and looked at the front of it he had recognized her scripted handwriting. Neat and tidy, every letter in its place, curves of the letters all tightly compacted in neat little loop to loops. Troy had slipped down the same alley way she had gone down. Opening the letter to read it.

He had stopped dead in the darkness and rain when he realized what the letter confessed. Face turning red and eyes darting back and forth as he had read each damning paragraph while his stomach rolled making him turn his face up to the pouring rain. How could she? She had betrayed him. It couldn't be possible, not his sweet dark twisted Ivy flower. Troy had shuddered and hung his head, dropping to his knees with the letter clenched in his fist. Rolling the other fist back and forth across his thigh. Troy had cried out as thunder rumbled through the air and a streak of lightning lit up the alley way.

He had spent what seemed an eternity weeping with his face turned up to the torrential downpour that seemed opened from the sky that night. Finally, when the last hitch of agony in his breath had subsided Troy tore apart Ivy's letter with a seething rage rolling across his face and body. He even left the confetti like pieces drifting in the rain water in the gutter that night too, spitting at them like they were little evil blanched demons sprouting out the dark, dirty water. He had stood up and stared into the darkness in the direction she had gone with a demented grin growing across his face. She would pay for this, soon, but he had to bide his time and make her pay in a way she would never forget – even in death. He had also found out quite quickly how deeply dark Ivy could be.

She was, surprisingly, his match and equal in almost every way he could have imagined, perhaps even surpassing and schooling him in some respects. Her penchant for hard, rough sex over top his prized doe had really taken him by surprise. Ivy had relished in the blood that had sprayed her face and body, slick with it she had become wild and unhinged, thrusting backward against him so hard that he had barely been able to hold on to her. It had been a carnal almost animalistic kind of sex. It seemed to be a primal rebirth for Ivy somehow and he had just been along for the ride that night.

☙

Here, in this cavern of mirrors, the lonely hours tick by with no explanation of the 'when' or where this is. I am floating and yet firm, I am here and yet not. I touch my arm and find only loose skin attached to what was bone, there are bugs, and maggots, and dirt but I cannot tell if this is real, perhaps I am cracked again, cracked like I was but there is something out of reach. Something just unfamiliar, if I am dead, then it is not possible to see what I am seeing, but if I am living the same is true.

Perhaps, if I could sleep but no something is ticking, something is twitching, something is clawing. What I can't tell now is why it's all so fuzzy. Why is it so dark here? What is that? I can't make sense of it all, I feel like I am falling, but then there is his voice, he is calling me, Ivy, my love, come closer, feel that, take this, its wet, its dark, you will like it. Come play"

I did enjoy it, whatever it was. These memories are just flooding me back and forth, there is the car. His jacket, the smell, the room and this toe. Why in the fuck is it itching? There I am again, floating back, his chest pressed against me, his lips, the steam of what was twisting in the sheets, the throbbing heated desire that dripped from me, that lingers. Why can't I recall what happened between us? Why is it so hard for me to know what time it is?

I can still smell him on the pillow. My body was limp from the passion that we showered on the bed last night, my body still feeling him in me, and on me, gods Troy, I love you when you do that too me. Makes me all tingly, wanting to do that again, now, here, wherever, take me like that, destroy me. That is what your dark Ivy wants. Give it to me, tie me, bind me whatever you want. I give you all and everything of me. It's our love I feel and yet I look down and feel something. My hands are raw and red, as if I have been scrubbing things way too hard.

☙

They had both collapsed to either side of the dead doe between them, her peering over the top of the doe's head at him with this lustful grin, lapping up the blood off her fingers and palms of her hands. He had smiled back at her thinking this is the one, I've found THE ONE. The one he could share his work with and not have to worry about her ever turning her back on him or judging him with that look that was like fingernails on a chalkboard to him.

How he hated when people looked at his work and scoffed at it. He put so much effort into it, he detested, abhorred that ungrateful look. It filled him with a boiling rage that consumed every thought and feeling, leaving him reeling like a wild animal. Ivy didn't do that at all to him, in fact she embraced his work fully. Though, sometimes he wondered if she was simply willfully allowing herself not to see, smell or feel what was around her in the apartment.

He had started leaving hints of his work more willingly in the open for her to find. From trinkets that came from his precious doe's body to outright leaving a doe or two around the place. Sometimes he swore she looked right at them and saw nothing but then she would come out of left field at him like she did with that blood rebirth of hers the other night.

ɞ

This mirror that reflects now is the one that I dread most, it seems that he has his own, a mirror framed with gory bits of dolls. Hands, legs, the parts dangle on them like a sick twisted nursery carousel that turns in the winds that whip through here, just to make me colder. I feel clean, wet, like someone washed me.

I don't remember cleaning anything; "Ivy. Ivy, look closer", "Who's there?", "I don't see you, I can hear you, where are you?" I feel like I am walking in fog, this place is not clear. I can't see where I am, I call out again, "HELLO??"

I start feeling nervous, as no one answers. I reach out, and feel the air around me, I feel like I am moving towards a thing, but there in the fog, there is nothing, I am nowhere, I am alone. I feel cold, I reach my arms rubbing them, but they feel wet, and do not heat my body from the cold. I find myself in a room, it's cold here, so very cold. There is a single chair, a table, a mirror, a cup, and paper, that is all. Where am I? "TROY???", "Please answer me??". " TROY" I scream out,sobbing, I collapse on the floor.

ɞ

"Did you hear me, my love?" Ivy asked, staring at him funny from across the restaurant table.

"Yes Ivy, I heard you," Troy spoke softly, "Okay, I'll show you what I do Ivy, I'll show you my work."

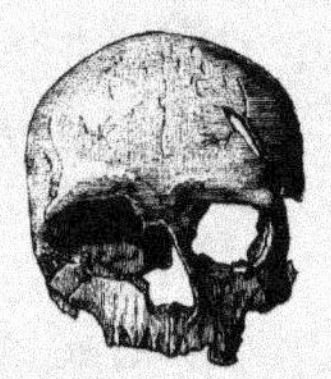

CARNIES AND CADAVERS

The place was a bit crowded, Troy hadn't expected a damn carnival in town. Its bright lights and annoying music on an endless loop. Ivy seemed enthralled with it all and Troy shook his head and had to smirk softly at the adorable wide-eyed stare she was giving. He nearly missed the doe while staring at Ivy, his deadly little flower. He smelt her first, the doe was wearing a scent that was light and creamy. Troy nuzzled into Ivy's shoulder and stole another glance toward the doe. Red hair and caramelized amber eyes. Ivory pale perfect skin. Ivy turned to Troy and looked at him with a puzzled look.

"Why are you looking at that red head like that?" Ivy asked him.

"You asked me to show you my work, she is a part of my work." He responded with a whisper in her ear.

"What the hell are you on about? Troy, you don't even know this girl." Ivy grunted with an indignant attitude. She stared hard at the red head, giving her a look that could run your blood cold. Ivy turned back to Troy with a warning look.

"Darling, I don't do threesomes if that's what you are after, I don't like sharing" Ivy growled.

"No love, not what I'm after. She is a prized doe for work, she is art waiting to happen" Troy grunted with his teeth bared at her. Troy was now slightly irritated with Ivy, she is smarter than this usually. It normally never takes Ivy much to realize what he wanted from her, but this was ridiculous.

...No, not that look, anything but that look...

Troy's feathers were now ruffled as Ivy stared at him wide eyed as the realization struck her full force. She tried to hide it though, Troy watched her pathetic attempt at recovering from the shock of understanding. Ivy shook her head to clear the cobwebs and something shifted across her face that took Troy by surprise. You could see the shift from shock to serious analytical thought then to acceptance of the whole idea.

Troy began to relax a little. Troy watched Ivy closely again looking for that look that made him seethe so badly. It was gone but the fact that it had been there at first troubled him gravely. She was scoffing at his work after all, just hiding it all this time. The letter that rainy night had proven that hadn't it. Troy gritted his teeth and forced a wide grin in Ivy's direction. Oh, how his heart ached, shattering into a million pieces. His precious flower has betrayed him. Troy's grin floundered a bit and he rolled his shoulders back and down, stuffing the pain deep into the core of himself.

☙

I see a letter, I feel the paper in my hand, so heavy, it tells everything about it, there is something I am missing, but the paper is there. It looks like my hand did this, but I can't recall, it's so frustrating. The fog, the table, the chair, the cup, nothing makes sense here. I feel something on my hands. It's sticky and dripping, something isn't right. I see a book, a diary, my words folded into it like eggs into batter, there is a hidden place, a place that holds something. I see a note, a letter, a plea and a photo, there are faces in there, and within those faces I found my primal self and screamed. I screamed, and screamed and the shades closed in and the mirrors laugh.

☙

"My precious Ivy be a dear and hand the red head one of my photography cards" Troy spoke as gently as he could while raising a brow at Ivy when she gave him a confused slack jawed look, "I meant artwork as in photography work my darling, what did you think I meant?"

ꕤ

As Ivy caught up to the redhead in the parking lot away from the crowds she stole a glance back toward Troy. He wasn't there, it startled Ivy that he was gone, and she tripped right into the redhead at her car. The photography business card loop de looped its way to the ground between the two women.

"I'm so sorry" Ivy kept repeating frantically.

"Hey, hey it's okay" the other woman said with a soft smile as she picked up the card and flipped it over.

ꕤ

Back into the mirrors. The past this time. The reflections again, pulling me back. Back into the place that haunted me. It's there that I am lost, lonely, stupid Ivy, the dead eyed doll. The room was dark, it was always dark there. My room where the stuffed animals guard the secrets of my scars, of the screams, the figures in the night, slipping slowly in and out of my room

I hear him, he is breathing. His hand strikes hard onto my face, he was doing it again, I was a bad girl, I was nothing. I am no good anymore, I am dirt, he told me that. I scream out "Daddy no" he does not stop." The belt comes out. I know what happens next, and still I look at myself in the mirror.

Little Ivy, innocence no more.

I am broken.

I am not the same.

It was these constant terrors in the dark, that walk with me, and what now strikes me to my core as the blade nicks at my wrist. Each cut a reminder that you are nothing, you feel nothing, you deserve to die. Back into the mirrors, this time forward, the past swirling, the future melting, time falls apart and again I am there, again I see him, I see Troy, I see my father, the faces.

They are all one, and the book, and the page, I see it, I see the hidden flap, I see where I placed in the glue, I see where I folded the note, corner to corner, this way, now folded, creased. I placed in the old photo.

☙

That's when it happened. It was so fast Ivy nearly screamed for the redhead who couldn't. Troy had appeared behind her with this look on his face. It was pure unadulterated rage rolling in waves off his body. There was this almost wild look in his eyes, Ivy couldn't quite place that look right away and gasped when she realized she was staring into the eyes of a predator. He bared his teeth and they looked almost razor-like as he growled while grabbing at the red head. He had something in his hand that he slapped over her mouth and nose. A rag of some sort.

When he started dragging the red head toward their car, her eyes rolling back, Ivy began to panic. Troy growled a warning at Ivy to pull her shit together and get in the car. At first, all Ivy could do was stare at her beloved Troy as if he was someone she didn't recognize. Then this cold chill ran down her back and spread from the core of her being out to the tips of her fingers, down her legs and into her toes. Up her neck and across her scalp into her face. A cold calmness overcame her and she stared into Troy's eyes as she slid into the driver's seat with her own teeth bared.

Troy tossed the car keys in her lap as he hopped into the passenger seat then turned to look at her. He studied her face for what seemed like an eternity. When he seemed satisfied with what he was looking for he told Ivy to crank the key and hit the highway, that he would guide her to where they were going.

"After all, you asked to see my work Ivy," Troy grunted, "I will show you my work."

"Where is she Troy?" Ivy whispered, afraid to speak any louder.

"In the trunk of the car, just drive Ivy."

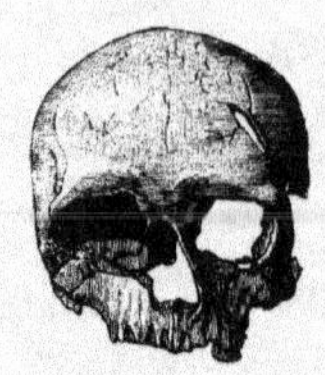

THE DEVILS IN THE ART

"Don't miss the dirt road Ivy." Troy told her curtly.

She did miss the road by a full two feet and had to slam the car in reverse and back up to pull into the dirt road. Troy laughed wildly when she missed it, howling with laughter deep from his gut. Ivy growled indignantly, was this their first fight? Ivy slammed the car to a full stop and turned toward Troy. How dare he laugh at her.

"That's not funny Troy," Ivy tried to keep her voice to an even keel but ended up hissing the words through gritted teeth, "You have never treated me like this before, Why now? What did I do?"

Troy cringed and hung his head while shuddering in his seat. He struggled between the utter sadness that ripped his heart into pieces and the rage that racked his body and coiled it like a viper getting ready to strike. His precious Ivy was poison to him, she had turned on him. How, how could this have happened, how did he miss it? She would pay for this, he would make her pay in the worse way possible.

"I'm sorry Ivy," Troy whispered softly while reaching for her across the seats, "you're right, I behaved poorly and I'm sorry my love."

Troy pulled her into his lap, kissing her forehead, both her eyes, then cheeks and mouth. Ivy, at first, didn't reciprocate but warmed to him after a moment or two. Kissing back, darting her tongue into his mouth then playfully nipping his lip. Troy gasped softly, sliding his hand under her skirt and tugging at her lace panties, breaking them away from her body.

I found the monsters that feed me this narrative, again and again, they stripped me from the good Ivy and left only the jagged rocks of a girl no longer innocent but forged into a disheveled husk. Each partner I chose, was one that reflected back to me those nights when I was little, the hot steaming pain of each strike, bruised and bleeding, my heart, my soul. Do you love me now daddy? Am I what you hoped for? LOOK AT ME. I am the result of you. You made me this. I am, with this knife, the monster that you forged. Troy.

Troy was not to blame for Ivy, no, he only saw what was broken in me. In a different life, I would have taken these scars to a place of light. I would have found a way to be a better Ivy, but the darkness was my chamber of solitude and in that chamber, he found me, he embraced me and the monster I was. I became a toy for him to foster, I was the product built to perfection. Ivy 2.0 and she was not the innocent one anymore. She was his and his alone and thus I give you. The makings and reasons for me.

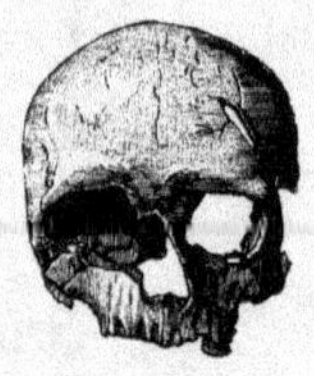

THUMP. THUMP. THUMP

Ivy jumped right out of her skin. For a moment she had forgotten the red head was in the trunk. Troy was staring at her with a wide lopsided grin on his face and a sparkle in his eyes. Ivy's own eyes roamed from his face to his chest where his breath heaved in and out, he was excited, aroused even. The hard heat in the crotch of his pants confirmed that he was aroused. More so than she had ever seen him before. It stirred a strange guilty warmth in her abdomen that snaked down between her legs, making her squirm.

"No time, my love, for pleasure, there is work that needs to be done first" he whispered as he kissed her on the mouth while she whimpered in protest.

Troy slipped out from underneath Ivy and slid into the driver's seat. He would take them the rest of the way. The dirt road here, in the dark, was dangerous and they couldn't afford to roll the car over in the bush at night. Not with a precious doe in the trunk at any rate. It's time to show Ivy what his work was about, then he had to work out how to make her pay for scoffing at that work.

ঙ

Ivy was sure now that Troy didn't suspect what she knew now. She seemed to have gotten away with hiding her horrifying realization that Troy was a serial killing lunatic. How had she not seen it before? She stared out the passenger window, feet up on the seat while hugging her knees tight.

THUMP. THUMP. THUMP

Ivy came to a horrifying second realization, she couldn't help the redhead in the trunk of his car. She would have to feign her way through this whole thing. She would have to witness a woman dying while a crazed lunatic took her life with a sadistic satisfaction. She should have listened to that oh so familiar letter more closely. She had thought it was a crazy ex girlfriend who had sent it, trying to break her and Troy apart.

She had been willfully blind to his activities around the apartment and his long excursions without her. She fingered the locket around her neck and almost didn't gag down the vomit that rose sourly to the back of her throat. Oh my god, her eyes widened, and she whined softly against the window. Troy grit his teeth as he cranked the music to a high crescendo, deafening them both and drowning out the thump-scream from the trunk of the car. He took the left bend turn hard, clipping the back of the car against the three birch trees that he normally narrowly missed.

...cold bones, yeah that's my love,

she glides away, like a ghost...

THUMP. THUMP. THUMP

Troy cursed under his breath and cranked the wheel the opposite way to catch the reverse S bend toward the bunker. There, the door at last. He brought the car to a screeching halt causing Ivy to lurch forward and slam the heel of her hand on the passenger dash. Her feet made an oddly satisfying plop on the floor of the car.

"Let's go Ivy, get out of the car." Troy told her, "We have work to do."

"Troy, please. Can't we just go home now." Ivy whispered softly, nuzzling up to him.

Troy yanked her roughly away from his body and stared her in the eyes, teeth bared menacingly. He turned her around and pressed the keys into her hand while shoving her toward the back end of the car. Tonight, he would guide her hands in her debut work of art. She just needed a push in the right direction.

Tonight, two would become one, he would take her here and reshape her into his dark and deadly Ivy. He would make her his finally. No more games, no more playing around, Troy thought to himself as he growled an instruction at Ivy.

"Careful, she's feisty. The feisty ones are troublesome sometimes." Troy growled. "Be prepared."

"Troy, I don't know if I can do this, please." Ivy whimpered.

"Move it." Troy grunted as he yanked the keys back from her with a sigh and popped the trunk suddenly.

The redhead sprung like a wild jack rabbit from the trunk of Troy's car, yowling loudly and taking wide sweeping strikes at the air between her and them. She was throwing her punches wild and cockeyed without even looking. Probably praying she makes some sort of connection, Troy smirked side stepping a wild right hook. There was a thud and Ivy was sprawled on her back with her cheek throbbing suddenly. The redhead made contact after all, Troy mused.

Ivy felt the wave of rage building in the center of her body, she shuddered and glared up only to see the redhead being led from the back of the neck by Troy to a door. A door in the middle of the woods? Ivy cocked her head to one side curiously, now she had seen it all. Why was she not surprised in the least?

Ivy yanked herself to her feet and rubbed her stinking cheek. She looked up and made eye contact with the redhead. Her mouth split into a wide, predatory grin. Her teeth gritting back and forth and fingers rubbing her now bruising cheek. Bitch is going to pay for that. The click of the lock startled both women for a moment and the door to the bunker swung inward. Troy flicked a switch and the droning hum of a set of halogen lighting cranked to life.

The lighting made the corridor of the bunker eerie. It made Ivy's hairs stand on end. She swore she saw something pass in front of them, in the dark shadows. Ivy could almost hear whispers, she gave her head a shake trying to rationalize the whispers as the scuffing of their shoes on the concrete floor of the corridor. You're imagining things Ivy, pull your shit together, there's nothing there. The redhead screamed and tried to pull away from Troy, but she only succeeded in making him furious. He slapped her then shoved her up against the wall of the bunker. Pinning her to it.

There was an audible shick and a flash of what looked almost like liquid silver then the redhead's shirt fell away from her body revealing her black lacy bra underneath. Troy gyrated against the redhead's rear, pressing hard and letting off a low deep moan.

Ivy's eyes widened as she growled "What the fuck Troy."

Troy looked up just in time to catch Ivy's hand before she could grab his switchblade from him. The redhead managed to slip out from under him as he moved away to catch Ivy's hand. Good thing I locked the bunker door back there. Troy looked past Ivy, watching the redhead run down the corridor and slam against the door at the end. He howled laughter as she scrambled with the handle of the door, scratching and pawing at it desperately.

He looked back at Ivy and raised a brow at her as if to say, go get her. Ivy cringed back at first then turned on her heel abruptly. She nearly screamed herself when a hand reached over her shoulder and stopped her in her tracks. Troy turned her around to face him again. He stared into her eyes making her shift uncomfortably from one foot to the other. She was about to ask him what the hell he wanted when she felt the cold hard shaft of the switchblade being pressed into her hand.

"Ivy, my love, bring her back here but cut away her clothes as you do," Troy purred softly in her ear, "bring her to me, naked as the day she was born."

Ivy couldn't help it, she moaned softly as she fingered the switchblade in her hands. Turning it this way and that then looking up at Troy. He nodded back at her and she turned back to the redhead. The precious doe, his precious doe. She had to go get the doe, like a good little girl. Ivy started down the corridor while the precious doe mewled and whimpered in her direction.

"You've been a very bad little doe." Ivy hissed as she sashayed down the corridor. She dragged the tip of the switch blade along the wall as her head slowly rocked from side to side. She eyed her prey with a wild shit eating grin and swirled the blade in the air in front of the doe's face.

"Please, help me." The redhead whimpered trying to grasp at Ivy, "please Ivy,"

Ivy bore her teeth and what came from her throat had no resemblance to the soft spoken and sweet Ivy that most people knew her as. This was the dark and twisted Ivy, the Ivy that could choke you one handed while laughing hysterically in your face. How dare this little bitch let my name roll off her stupid little tongue. I'm going to rip that tongue out and shove it down her throat. Ivy lunged at the doe, grabbing her by her red curls and yanking her to her knees.

She was going to make this bitch bleed, she would make her pay for that little taunt with Troy back there. Thinking she could get a little something from her man.

Bitch was going to regret stepping into her territory that's for sure. Ivy rolled her head from side to side, taking a deep breath. She had to be smart about it. Troy had asked her to bring the doe back to him naked. Ivy knew she and Troy would make the doe pay. She just had to be patient didn't she? Ivy pulled the precious doe gently to her feet, nuzzling the red head's face with her own. The red head relaxed a little letting Ivy get a little closer.

"There, sweet precious," Ivy cooed softly, "it's okay, put your head on my shoulder sweetheart."

"Thank you." The doe whispered, "Please don't let him hurt me."

"Oh, he isn't who you need to worry about." Ivy grinned maniacally at the doe as she swiped the blade under the red head's belt.

The sound of the belt giving under the sharp blade was surprisingly satisfying to Ivy. She hadn't thought there could have been anything more satisfying to her ears. Ivy heard Troy shift behind her and felt the hardness of his manhood press into her bottom. She would make him wait like he made her wait in the car. Ivy pushed him back, waving him away and making him smile while he stepped back for her. She popped the button on the doe's pants with the switch blade and tugged at the zipper.

Letting the red head's pants hit the floor with a soft swish. Ivy nuzzled the whimpering woman, making her stand straight as she pulled first her bra roughly over the doe's head and then her panties down her legs to her ankles.

"Step out of them like a good little precious," Ivy whispered, "be a good little doll."

The redhead did as she was told, trembling and trying to hide her nakedness from both Troy and Ivy with her hands. Ivy looked back at Troy, his eyes sparkled, and his hand rubbed at his manhood, he was outright panting now. Ivy smirked at him and took the doe by the hand as she walked the red head back down the corridor toward him.

"Christ," Troy moaned as Ivy pressed the redhead against him. He turned the precious doe toward the wooden door at the end of the hallway. "Start walking my little doll."

Ivy giggled as she twirled the silver switchblade around. Watching the halogen lighting sparkle and twinkle off the hilt of the blade. Something moved beyond her vision and past the blade. She looked and had to cringed backward, nearly tripping over her own feet. She slapped a hand to her wide-open mouth to keep the scream from escaping. There in the darkness was a face, slices up and down the cheeks. The mouth pulled into a grotesque perverted permanent smile with staples and stitching. The eye lids were missing on this woman's face. Her silvery grey eyes staring woefully into Ivy's deep emerald ones.

Look what you helped him do. How could you?

Ivy tried to gag back the hot putrid vomit rising in her throat. It was no use, she no longer had control over her own stomach and it's urgent need to empty itself. Ivy felt the sting of bile as she heaved and wretched the contents of her gut all over the wall and floor of the corridor. The face came closer to hers, rising between the wall and her, materializing through her stinking vomit pouring from her mouth. Those eyes staring deeply into Ivy's, staring into the very core of her being.

Come back home Ivy. We are all waiting for you.

"Ivy." Ivy jolted at the sound of his voice. It was loud and stern in the cramped corridor. The smell of damp earth and rotting leaves with her steaming hot vomit on the ground made Ivy wretch again and she slapped her hand on the wall to steady herself. Her other hand had a death grip on the hilt of the switchblade. She looked up and again nearly screamed but this time at the icy blue eyes she had come to love losing herself in. Troy had this odd look on his face, Ivy couldn't quite figure out what that look was, then it dawned on her as she rasped a forced giggle out of her raw throat.

He was uncertain, confused. Ivy would even guess unsure. She had never seen him not sure of himself. Uncertainty was not in Troy's vocabulary. He touched her face, lifting it to look her in her eyes. Troy swiped a lock of her jet-black hair away from her face and unbuttoned his shirt. He pulled it off and wiped her brow and face then mouth with it.

It was as tender a gesture as a lunatic could possibly make, or was it mimic, and it made Ivy guiltily swoon all that much more for Troy. He may be a lunatic serial killer but wasn't he her lunatic serial killer as much as she was his dark little Ivy. She forced the thoughts from her mind and straightened herself, pushing off from the wall shakily.

"I'm okay, just the excitement of the night." Ivy managed through her sourly raw throat.

Troy frowned, a deep furrow in his brow forming. How oddly sudden, she seemed to have seen something too, I wonder what it was Troy thought. Troy had already knocked the new doe out a second time and placed her in the room beyond the wooden door. He had to go back for Ivy because she had lagged behind him. When he had reached her she had already been dry heaving with a strange look on her face, like she'd seen a ghost or something.

Ivy was looking at him with a tenderness that made him shiver delightfully. He pulled her close to him, kissing her forehead and taking her hand to slide it between his legs. When she gripped the bulge there it made him tilt his head back and shudder a long, deep growling moan.

It was like a million tiny little deaths when his sweet Ivy caressed him like that, the tingling prickly feeling as his breath came in heavy and fast. She started off gentle and ended rough with a strong squeezing grip that made him both shake with excitement and shivered as a twinge of pleasurable pain buried itself deep in his groin. What a fine line of pain and pleasure. The sweet caress of fingers combined with the hard pull. It made him bite his own lip and draw blood. Ivy pulled away while peering over Troy's shoulder.

She gasped, wide-eyed and astonished. What lay beyond him was a room. The light hummed miserably over a shiny table. The kind of table you would see in a coroner's morgue. It was shiny, and the red headed doe was laying on it. Beside the table was another table with odd looking instruments on it. Ivy knew what a scalpel was but that bigger one that was wide, the name of it eluded her right now. Bone something or other. Her eyes roamed, and she croaked a startled grunt. A mirror. It caught her face in its reflection and threw it back at her. Beyond the mirror was a wall full of shelving.

On that shelf were mason jars. So many mason jars Ivy marveled. She slowly tiptoed into the room, almost resembling a little mouse in a field as she crossed the threshold of the door. In those mason jars. My god, was it? It is? Bones, floating in an odd fluid in each of the jars. Some had small trinkets with the bones, bobbing in that strange clear brownish liquid.

Other jars had an eyeball or an earring with the bones. Ivy gazed at the shelves of bone jars, staring at them in pure childlike awe. How many were there, how long has he been doing this? Each jar had its own label, meticulously and lovingly labeled in a neat, tight cursive writing. That is Troy's writing! Ivy touched one of the jars and let off a strangled whimper, 'that' jar label had her writing on it. No, no she didn't, she couldn't have. Ivy backed up into the cadaver table behind her causing the red head to moan softly and weakly flail her hands.

Troy turned Ivy around to face the precious doe. The red head's eyes fluttered as Ivy moaned softly when Troy slipped his hand into her shirt. He pushed her over the table, pressing himself to her. Ivy stared into the doe's face as Troy pushed her skirt up over her hips.

"I'm taking you here Ivy, spread your legs" Troy breathed heavily

"Not here, Troy, no, why can't we go back to the bed at home" Ivy moaned

"No, my love, not there, here is where I want my dark Ivy, you are mine now, bend over like a good girl and smile love smile, you are mine now love, mine alone"

What was it about the smell that was familiar, I recall the feeling of thrusting something, a cold wet liquid spilling on me, but it was not his. There was a whimper, a sigh and there I was, writhing over the sound, riding over the wave of the smells, the sounds the feeling of cold. I slump over a table, Troy shoving my skirt over my hips, "I am taking you here Ivy, spread your legs"

I give and consent to him, riding his hardness with a pleasure I have never known, I am in ecstasy, he lifts me slightly, bouncing my round bottom off his manhood, I was surrounded by him, whimpering, and gripping the table.

"Ivy, you are helping me, do it for me my love, twist her good" Troy breathed heavily in Ivy's ear with each thrust of his hips.

Ivy gripped the table as the climax ripped through her body in waves. She cried out just as the doe started screaming. Her hands did the work for her, the shick of the blade, the rip of skin and the splash of coppery hot red liquid slapping Ivy full in the face. Ivy screamed her pleasure and Troy's name as he arched his back with a low rumbling moan of his own. His thrusts became wild and erratic, his manhood stiffening as Troy bounced Ivy's round bottom, banging her thighs hard against the cadaver table. Ivy surrendered all of herself to his darkness embracing it as her own.

Becoming whatever he needed her to be. The dark, twisted little flower, his little Ivy flower. The doe struggled to breath through the gaping tear in her throat, mouth opening and closing like some odd half human, half fish thing. It was wholly irritating to Ivy suddenly and she felt a cruelty seep into her heart, god this bitch couldn't even die quietly either.

"Die you stupid bitch." Ivy hissed through clenched teeth pushing herself up from the doe. There was a sound like metal on metal and Ivy panicked, where did the switchblade go, her hands groping around for the silvery hilt. Troy leaned in and held her hands to the table with one of his. Sliding something under them. The switchblade! Ivy drew a shaky breath and relaxed.

The doe beneath her was now cooling off, her death rattle slowing to nearly nothing but a gasp here and one there. The blood dripping off Ivy's face was starting to congeal and clot on her forehead and cheeks. Her hands were thick with the doe's blood and Troy's seed mixed in. She stared at her hands for a long time, watching the crimson blood turn to a deeper red then a sickly brown on them. What had she done Ivy thought as tears started rolling down her cheeks creating tracks in the drying blood on her face.

What have I done? Ivy tossed her head back and froze staring into her own deep green eyes in the mirror. She didn't recognize herself anymore, this wasn't her anymore.

☙

"Ivy, the mirror. Look, it's time now" a voice reaches out to me, I search for it but it is not there, I can hear it, and without knowing why I pick up the mirror. What I see is not me. What is happening. Oh my god why am I losing myself. TROY, WHERE ARE YOU!!! I am panicked. I cannot find him, my heart is racing, I pick up the mirror, and in there is us. Our apartment, but what is this? What did I do?

Looking down now at my hands it all comes into play. There in the mirror, we were that night, ridding pleasure like a never-ending wave, back and forth in the deep and dark places only known to that which holds my intimate places, cradling them with care, he honors them like a jewel and worships at the temple of my secret places for which he is the high priest. That is not water, it is blood. It's clear to me the thing that I am riding on is one of his doe's, he is fucking me on her as if she is nothing. This is the last of what I am, the last part of me that was clinging on in denial.

Then the memories become clear. Looking into that mirror, I see who I am, Oh Ivy, what are you now? There on our first night, there on the bed in which I loved him his toys lay under the bed rotting like raw meat. The smell becomes clear, the house is laid with stains of that which has left its mark, the claws in the floor, the bits of blood and teeth that spew up into the sink. I am suffocating. I feel it now. Ivy, you are a killer aren't you.

I recall now what that feeling was that night. It was the knife in my hands, he told me, Ivy just do it. You are helping me, my love. Come on he said in his honey voice, do it for me, twist her good. The blade went into her like butter.

Blood soaking us both, and he fucked me in it, right there, the feelings of blood, the puddle, it was more than I could take, but if I was good at all, or even possibly in the light still, I would have run from this place, but no, he knows me too well, I am like him. I am not Ivy anymore. I am his creation.

The time slips from me, as corpse after corpse piles up like stacks of paper, one on the other, I begin to lose whatever I have left, I tell this one "shut up, and die", I become deeper and darker, losing myself in Troy, in his heat, in this sickness, I want to be doing this don't I? I want to put this mirror down, I don't want to look, but my hand, it's stuck.

I cannot help it, I am forced to obey, forced to look. There again, those nights in darkness, ridding me, holding me, twisting and turning me over and over, the memories flooding back and forth and I am here, and I am there, and it is cold, so cold. I cannot see myself, in this thing, only the apartment, only the bodies, only the squealing, wrenching sounds of the doe's wide open throats then me and Troy and the writhing agony. It got to me. Like a festering wound I could not continue to be like him, it was because I grew afraid.

Seeing how deep and dark he was, I may have hurt them too, but not like him. I wanted to spare them, he wanted to prolong it. I couldn't anymore. I wrote it down, I walked in the rain, I left the letter in a box by the door of a police station, I ran, .how did he know, but I know now, he was following me. Stalking me. His Ivy could not look at him anymore, she was scared, I was scared, I wanted out and that night there was dinner, there was the last night and now here I am. Wherever this here is.

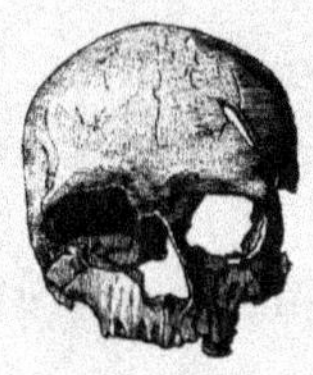

POISONED LITTLE FLOWER

The nausea overcame Ivy again, her stomach rolled and recoiled. Ivy started gagging violently as Troy was washing up at the utility sink. He looked over at Ivy and watched with mild curiosity. He brought Ivy a cup and a cloth. The cup had a warm liquid in it and it smelled so good. Ivy sipped gingerly at it, her eyes peering over the lip of the cup at her beloved Troy. He smiled softly, offering the cloth to Ivy. It too was warm, and Ivy relished it as she started wiping her face and neck with it. Troy was such a darling, always thinking of her. Troy seemed oddly quiet though. Keenly watching her every move.

Ivy watched him pick up the scalpel and cock his head to one side. A quick flick of his wrist and the doe's smile was widened into an awful gaping grin. The sound of the staple gun made Ivy nearly jump out of her skin. With thread and needle, Troy made the final adjustments and the doll's gruesome smile was now complete. She had gone from doe to doll in the matter of a few flicks of his wrist. Ivy leaned heavily against the table, grimacing as a cramp rolled through her guts. She started to pant and gag when another cramp followed quickly behind the other. Why was it so hard to catch her breath, why is it getting so cold? Ivy thought as she glanced over the edge of the table. She had knocked the cup over off the smaller table and the liquid was running between her big toe and the one next to it.

She could swear her toe was starting to itch. Ivy looked up at Troy and croaked a whimper at him. He was standing over her staring down at her. His face twisted in a rueful smile while he twisted the scalpel between his thumb and finger. The light of the halogen gleaming off the sharp edge of the scalpel blinding Ivy.

"My sweet little Ivy flower," Troy whispered as he bent to catch her eyes with his, "you broke my heart you know that. You didn't appreciate my work. You tried to ruin it by writing that letter. Why, Ivy. We were so good together and you were my sweet twisted little Ivy."

Ivy moaned deep in her throat and stared back down at the cup. No, it wasn't a letter from an ex girlfriend. It was her letter to the police. He must have been following her around. She hadn't gotten away with it after all. Ivy looked back up at Troy, searching his face for some left-over hint of love or passion, something she could lean in on, maybe use to survive with. There was nothing, Ivy sighed heavily and hung her head as she resigned herself to what was to come.

"Troy, what was in the cup?" Ivy asked as another cramp in her gut caused her to lean into the table and groan, "What did you give me?"

"Oh, my sweet twisted Ivy." Troy hissed, "You were poisoned to me, so I poisoned you with, of all things, your very name, Poison Ivy."

Ivy started gasping for breath, her heart thudding in her chest. Rattling her rib cage and racing it's final laps. Ivy moaned as her gut rolled and she threw open her mouth. Frothy vomit streaked with bile and blood flowed from her mouth and onto the floor. Her head spun, and her heart thudded against her chest again. Ivy stumbled forward, and Troy caught her tenderly. He pulled her close to him and put her head on his chest.

"It's alright my little Ivy flower," Troy purred as he kissed her forehead, "time to rest my love."

Ivy rolled her head to one side and her eyes caught in the mirror again. Her green eyes staring into themselves, roaming over a face she no longer could begin to recognize or understand. Ivy's chest heaved as she shuddered the last breath of life out into Troy's shoulder and she closed her eyes to finally rest.

ଓ

The mirror fades to my face, I finally see me. I am not the Ivy I was, my face or what remains of it a haunting memory, and I finally understand. I see someone walking towards me, a woman smiles at me reaches out her hand

"Forgiveness is this way, my dear." She says. She takes me to a room, there I am in the void, around me circles our dolls.

"Ask them for forgiveness," she says, "and mean it."

"Please forgive me." I sob into the darkness

They come closer, surrounding me, they hold me, I feel something, they take out their knives, this time it is for me, I surrender to them just like Troy, I am nothing now, nothing but the dark black earth. Nothing but these bones. Nothing but that piece of tooth you see in that jar. I am there, my story is one of many, we are in these jars together, waiting to be free. There was a time when I was innocent, all around me there was love and care and hope.

I don't know how that was lost, it was not my music, I am not insane, I have never hurt anyone before. Yet there was something, wasn't there? This darkness in me, growing like cancer. Troy is not to blame for finding that, I let him. I let him take me, touch me, penetrate me, and in the safety of his arms there was crumpled, dead and there left bare the deepest darkness. It was always the blood.

The blood, the feeling of it. I can see it on my arm as a girl, the cuts, the coping, the silent reminders of the covering of the pain. The sobbing, the darkness, my heart broken and shattered like glass. They took it from me, my innocent heart. There in the dark, my wrist painfully scared from the flimsy blade, releasing the pain, why could I not take this pain into the light? Why did it push me to darkness?

I, Ivy, admit fully, that I do not think everyone becomes like me, but there is always something in us, that chooses the light or the dark there is no middle, there is no semblance of grey, we are either drawn to live in the sunshine or the darkness, and I fell in the abyss, like a dying star, I gave way to it, and it engulfed me. I should have never let them silence me, the silence was deafening for me, I felt things, heard things, I was not whole anymore, and life just went on.

My scars were that which made this Ivy whole and yet broken. When Troy saw them he knew I was like him, even though his wrist did not bear the brunt of my secrets he knew, that this shattered fragile little bird could be wrought into the darkness, for she was seeking it out, and in him she found it. He knew what was in me, and if by any other circumstance, I met anyone else that day, I could be Ivy the well-rounded suburban housewife instead of this.

This disgusting mass of decaying flesh, bone protruding over the skin. My dress hangs from me like oiled cloth, I am rotting and unnatural, I am what you see in the dark on Halloween, I am not Ivy anymore, but a shell. Troy knew me, he knew that shell was waiting to be filled and he filled it. Not just filled it, but reformed that shell-like clay, he molded me. His precious Ivy, his creation, his desire. I was his masterpiece and yet in the end, it was me. I am that which took him down, and for that you should understand that this means some part of me deserves redemption, even though I know you will not grant it.

Why should I expect anything other than the women who kill, you understand nothing about them, how much do you expect us to take. There are things in us that force us to commit unspeakable acts, and in that you will never understand what it is like to have all that is in you taken until all you have is a black, decaying heart, where no light can reach, and that heart finds another just like it.

Someone who whispers understanding, acceptance, one who is there to comfort you and mold you, but yet this other half is as rotten as you, perhaps even more so, and your hopes lay bare on a mountain of decaying bones with only the scars of what you have done reminding you of what you did.

You cannot erase it, you cannot remove it, you face it, and know you did that, you became the thing that all fear, you become death.

So, when the knife went into my hand, slicing them this way and that, he was slicing me. I was killing me, I wanted to end myself and Troy knew. He knew that even in my normal perfection I was inside a shell. Judge me if you want, I would. Seeing them dying on me, the blood, the knife, these bones in the jar. They tell my story, and theirs. The ivy that was is no more and yet they will not weep for me, because I killed and to tell you the truth I liked it.

The cold is now something I am, I understand why I felt it so harshly, I understand now why I cannot satiate my desires, corpses do not get that. We don't get the comforts of life, but instead get only the reminder of what we have done. The doe's now around me, those fragile hands that took their pound of flesh, that stabbed what was left of this decaying husk, they deserve peace, and I hope they find it. I walk these halls, while my bones sit on his mantle, and I wait for him.

However my love, when you find your Ivy, I hope you know this time your monster, your creation, is coming for you. There was in the distance the sound of a blade, sharpening itself on the stone. The knife is waiting, it's ready, it calls out and says "Come play with me".

The knife is there, it's ready and it sings to me. It calls me, there it is, my little darling, my little friend. It's cold steel waiting. The blade is the only comfort now, my only solace. It has taken the place of my precious stuffed animal, it has become what holds my secrets. This blade, she is my only release, she knows me, maybe she is an extension of me, this bitter, cold, and hopeless blade. She is waiting to find her resting place, and she is hungry.

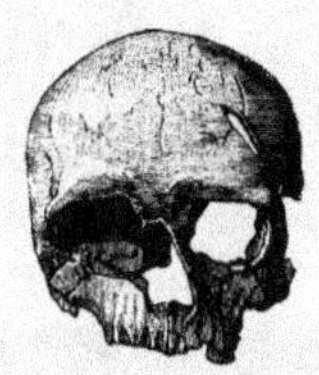

IS THAT MR. AGENT MAN?

The bathroom door was slightly ajar, the shower running and steam pouring out the crack of the door. A soft whistling of a tune drifting lazily along with the steam from the shower. He wasn't the biggest guy on the profiler team at the FBI special crimes unit, or agent for that matter. Not by a long shot but he had proven that you didn't need to be the biggest to be the bad ass in the team either. Stepping out of the shower he caught a glance of himself in the mirror.

The tattoo was extensive. Running from the left side of his back, wrapping around his left set of ribs and over his shoulder and down his left arm. They hid something a little more sinister on his skin and from his past. An accident, he had been the only survivor, but it had left him with extensive physical wounds that had healed into scars, but the psychological ones would never quite heal.

The one part of the tattoo was a samurai, face mask violently pulled away and a geisha's hand firmly planted on the warriors shoulder. His sword was drawn down the inner forearm and 7-5-3 brandished across the blade. The geisha reached from his back to the samurai where her touch squarely landed on both his and the samurai's shoulder. She was his temperance, his patience, his purpose and honor.

His ribs bear a tattoo matching the samurai's own armor across them. It was a symbol of a way of life mostly long forgotten except by a few select people like himself. Whistling the tune again, one he had heard not that long ago, and had stuck like the ear worm that it was, the man wiped the mirror in front of him meeting his own steely blue-grey eyes in it.

...if you bleed, I bleed the same...

He picked up the brush and ran it through his wavy shoulder length black hair. He was thinking about the file that hit his desk yesterday. The crimes in that file were the work of a serial killer across several states. All women victims. Faces gored and disfigured, stapled and stitched into a grotesque version of a smile. Some had been violently ripped apart, as if the killer had been enraged. Most though, treated tenderly. Almost lovingly. All the victims had the same thing in common though, pieces of bone and teeth missing from the corpses.

Some had both fingers and toes missing. Some only a few fingers. All had teeth missing. Their bodies scrubbed clean with disinfectant and left in open areas. The agent suspected they were left out in the open because the killer wanted them found, like pieces of art. The killer was an ambush killer, he used chloroform to subdue his victims from behind. Where he took them after that was a mystery still, but the agent and his team knew where they found the bodies was a secondary crime scene.

The killer's dump sites. There was something else that was a mystery too, the last dozen or so victims the modus operandi had changed drastically. It seemed, their killer may have picked up a partner in crime. The killer's partner was confusing even to the agent, delicate hand yet sometimes a heavy hand with the way the cuts had been made in the last dozen plus victims. Almost like this crime partner wanted to spare as much pain as possible but couldn't help indulging in causing as much pain as possible too. It was all over the place. The agent suspected the killer's new partner was still evolving, growing more confident at every new kill. The reason the file had hit his desk was because the second killer had a similar M.O to one of his other cases.

One that had plagued him for years now. One that had almost cost him his job in the early days. A soft rap at the bathroom door tore the man's attention away from his thoughts. He looked over with a soft grunt and put his brush down on the ledge of the sink.

“What is it?” He was irritated at the disruption of his thoughts.

“There’s another victim Agent Desbrates”

“For fucks sake, do we have any details yet?”

“Yes, it’s a dark haired, female victim. Green eyes and dressed in plaid slacks and a white blouse. She was placed, not dumped in the middle of a park and Agent Denver, this one’s very different. Fingers missing, teeth and this time eyes missing but no disfigurement, hair brushed even. Seems she was treated well. Bloody foam in the throat and mouth suggests she suffocated somehow says the C.S.I unit on the scene now.” The other agent replied.

Agent Desbrates, Leo stared into the mirror. Damn. Sounds like they had another change in motive and modus operandi. This case was proving to be a royal pain in Leo’s ass just like the asylum case was and is. These, now two killers, were leaving a bloody fucking path across several states and the team was trailing painfully behind.

“I’ll be out in a few minutes, make sure no one screws up my crime scene and we can head there asap.” Leo spat out.

He looked back into his own steely blue-gray eyes and cursed these two, swearing he would catch them even if it meant he had to sacrifice a pound of flesh and blood to do it. Looking at the samurai’s face on his shoulder Leo bore his teeth for a moment then rolled his shoulders and started to whistle that infernal damn tune again as he got dressed.

...If you’re scared, I’m on the way...

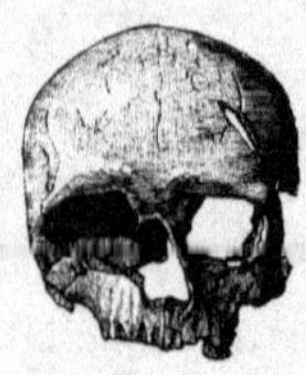

IN THE PARK, THERE WAS THIS LADY

The park was quiet as the sun rose with hues of red, yellow and orange. The light crept across the body marking time as it passed slowly. The empty sockets where the eyes were meant to be were dark and foreboding, beckoning to anyone to look closer for their truth of the matter. Her dark black hair was brushed neatly and tenderly over her right shoulder. The white blouse was, obviously, put on after she had died, same for the plaid slacks. The difference, Agent Desbrates noted as he crouched beside the body, was glaring, no ghastly mock of a smile with the mouth stitched closed and cut artificially wide.

"LEO"

Leo twitched and grimaced. Gods he hated that woman sometimes. Agent Bast was a brooding and tall Egyptian American woman with a hard-lined jaw and thin hawk-like nose. Her eyes were as steely blue-grey as Leo's were with flecks of gold and silver in them. Her attitude was as hard lined as her facial features. Her voice was nasally and grated on Leo's nerves like a violin's bow on steel strings.

"Leeeooooo," Bast rumbled at him, "start talking to me, we need to coordinate here,"

Leo sniffed and shook his head as he sighed then rocked back on his boot heels. Bast may be a bitch but she was damn good at micromanaging a case into the solved pile. He would need her decidedly bitchy brains to help him with this case.

"It's the same killers Bast," Leo chucked in her direction as he looked up at the overbearing woman barreling a stare back down at him, "a bit different though if you couldn't tell. This one wasn't mutilated and was placed here rather than dumped unceremoniously."

"Well, let's get her to the coroner so we can get any prints and forensics off her before it opens up and pours holy hell down on us, clouds are rolling in. Don't forget to go over the scene as well Leo."

Leo growled. As if he would somehow arbitrarily "forget" to go over the crime scene with a fine-tooth comb. She just had to take that stab. He had been a rookie when he made that mistake a long time ago. Leo dropped his head low, thinking and mulling the new victim and crime scene over in his head. She had been sprawled out, arms wide and legs closed. Blouse perfectly set on her, each button done up from top to bottom, not a one missed.

Her hair over her right shoulder. Why right and not left? Or did it matter? The plaid pants looked like they'd come from a pant suit perhaps. The one cuff on the left had a small hole in them, as if it had been caught up on something. It looked like the perp had tried to smooth it over too. That told Leo it meant something to this perp that this victim be treated with the utmost respect, treated with delicacy and dignity. Did he know this woman perhaps? Old lover? New one? Leo stared at her empty eye sockets then leaned in closer.

"Someone get me tweezers and gloves! NOW"

The tweezers appeared in a set of latex free blue gloves, Leo slapped the gloves on with a snapping sound and reached with the tweezers into the victim's right eye socket. Slowly, he pulled out a crumpled piece of paper, or part of one at least. A bit of blood and body fluids soften one edge of the balled-up paper. Leo let the paper drop into the palm of his left hand then dropped the tweezers into the grass next to the victim's head. He gently undid the paper, there was a spiral like cursive writing on one side. Parts of words missing at the edges.

It looked like it had been torn apart in a pure rage. Words like "I wish I had recognized," and "...my part to play in..." Odd, Leo wondered as he brooded over the paper.

He stared down at the eyeless woman at his feet and cocked his head to one side. Who are you? He mused as he finally stood up, stretched then barked orders for the coroner staff to come get the DB and prep it for transport to the local morgue. Leo looked around the body one last time while the coroner's staff worked with the dead woman. The sound of the body bag zipper always made Leo shiver without fail. Leo noted that there were depressions in the grass, some had already been casted by the C.S.I team. You can see the plaster bits in the grass from it.

A quick estimate says a size 11 or 12 men's, loafers? Not sneakers or running shoes, this guy was way too classy for that. Not much else is at the scene evidence wise though. If there had been it would have been picked up by the team working the scene. Leo made a mental note to stop by the forensic lab and see what they had found. Leo's eyebrow raised and his hackles went up suddenly, his eyes darted around as he got the sense of being watched. It crawled up his back like lady death's fingers and made him shiver. Shaking it off he started barking new orders at the others on the scene, telling one to watch where they fucking stepped while moving another out of his way to talk to the coroner's field supervisor to make plans to be there for the autopsy.

☙

Troy grunted softly as he watched the agents yap back and forth. The guy was on his boot heels next to his precious Ivy as he looked up at the foreign looking woman beside him. Her features were sharp and didn't interest Troy very much, wasn't his type, too tall, too lanky. The man though, something about him that struck Troy oddly. Small for a man but fantastically built. Not bulky muscle but defined and ripped from what he could tell. This guy's face had some odd angles for a man though, softer but not.

The fact that they had found Ivy so quickly troubled Troy, he hadn't even had time to fix her pant cuff that he had caught on a snag from his trunk. Sorry my love, can't help that now. When the male agent yelled for tweezers and gloves Troy grinned from ear to ear. Snappy man this guy huh, he was a quick bugger wasn't he. Troy watched in amusement as the man examined the piece of ripped paper with a perplexed look on his face – maybe not as snappy as Troy thought then.

The man abruptly stood and started barking orders at the others around him, that was Troy's cue to take exit left. This agent and Troy had a later date at some point. He was sure of it as he was sure that the doe in his trunk was right at this moment. He was looking forward to meeting "Leo" soon but for now, Troy would leave them to his masterpiece that was his precious little Ivy flower. He had pressing artistic matters to attend to just now and as it stood, there was work to be done.

ଓ

Leo was muttering softly under his breath as he investigated the gaping black holes of the unidentified woman's face. He wondered what color her eyes might have been and if they'd find them for her to be whole again. The right eye socket was where he had found the piece of paper. Spiraling cursive on one side, words missing and bleeding past the edges. Such odd words to use like "my part to play in". Trailing off like a mysterious message in an invisible bottle. He scanned her face, silky smooth and white skin.

Looks like she took very good care of herself it seemed. Decay hadn't set in yet because they had found the body so quickly, so her cheeks were tight and not sunken in, yet. Leo brought his face close to hers, the smell of bleach and her shampoo wafted up to him. Staring into her hollowed out eye sockets he again wondered who she was, where she'd come from, what was she like, how had she lived. So many questions, if only the dead could speak in tones the living could hear.

"So, how goes it" a voice chimed in making Leo nearly jump out of his skin.

He looked up to see Ari staring back at him with her moody deep violet eyes. Leo wracked his brain trying to remember what she had said about why her eyes were violet like that, he had asked once for small talk. Be damned if he could... Alexandria's Genesis!! That's what it was, funny how things stuck in his head like that, weird little gems of facts that had no real rhyme of reason, just oddities that seemed to stick around. Leo had always been like that, a sponge of sorts for tidbits of information that were useless.

It was a blessing but also a curse at times because that useless tidbit sometimes turned out to be very useful. Leo cocked his head to one side and regarded the unidentified woman again then looked back up into the violet eyes staring at him impatiently. He was also good at annoying people with his slow, measured responses to them. Another blessed curse it seemed.

"It goes," Leo muttered, "slowly, but it goes."

"Well, at least it goes," Ari grunted as she slapped the clipboard on the desk a little too hard. Gods that man drove her to maddening frustrations. She side eyed Leo, looking him up and down as he continued to look over the dead woman on her table.

Ari smiled softly despite her frustration, he wasn't the tallest guy on the planet, in fact was below the average male height. He wasn't short and stout or anything like that, not in the least. He was well built for his tiny stature, strong looking. He was ripped underneath that suit, how did Ari know? Well, they had a thing way back. A torrid affair, racy and full of fireworks but full of fighting and hardships as well. He was a hard man to live with, he was set in his ways. Ari was much younger than him and stubborn in her ways as well. They had great sex but horrible relationship, they were better as friends really but damn he was so yummy. Ari smirked just as Leo looked up and caught her staring at him. He shook his head at her and tossed that hot lop-sided grin of his in her direction.

"Tell me about Jane Doe here." Leo chuckled as he unbuttoned his jacket and tucked his hands into his pant pockets. His shirt at the top was unbuttoned and showing a little skin and tattoo. His badge glistening in the hard morgue light while the revolver peeked its grip from behind his left hip. It made Ari's girly bits tingle a bit. What a god damn tease this man could be. She wondered if he knew that he was teasing.

"Ari?"

"Yes, yes. Jane Doe, sorry Leo," Ari grunted, "I haven't done much yet other than prepping, pulling some tissue samples and blood. Nothing under her nails, they were cleaned out like all the rest of them. Her hair was brushed so I suspect I won't find any debris or evidence there either. I suspect I'm not going to find much, like all the rest of them before her Leo."

"Do what you can darlin' and let me know the results of all the tests as soon as possible would you." Leo turned back to Jane Doe. He stared at those empty sockets again.

Lost in thought. Why would the killer stuff a piece of paper in her eye socket? Why the right one? This was not the same modus operandi of all the other victims. This one somehow, felt different, in some way. There was way more care put into this victim. Almost as if the killer had loved this one, really loved this one, had spent time with this one, quite a bit of it in fact. Leo's senses were tingling and screamed that this one was something special to the killer. Her makeup was done perfectly, not a single bit out of place.

She had been placed in her final resting spot. The killer had even tried to smooth out the torn part of her pant cuff. The paper had been placed delicately into the eye socket, not shoved in at all. Her blouse had been buttoned with the utmost care as well. Spotless, crisp and clean, dry cleaners? All the other victims had not been treated with this much care and love. Some had been dumped unceremoniously even. Faces unrecognizable and beaten to such a degree that they had to ask a forensic reconstruction team to build the skulls back up for any semblance of a recognizable face.

Her hair was left intact, none of the other victims had their hair left in place, hell it was brushed for fuck sakes. What was it about this one for the killer, what was different?

Leo pursed his lips and brought his face closer to the corpse's face, "Who are you?" He asked her quietly as if she'd be able to answer at all. All Leo got was the emptiness of black holes where her eyes had been, staring at him silently. How god damn maddening.

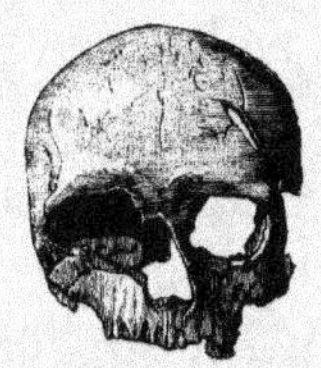

THE SOUND OF INEVITABILITY

Troy stood in the middle of his forest. Listening to the muffled woman in his car sob and plead with him to let her go. ***Why*** do they always have to beg like that, it's irritating. Fucking whiny bitch. Troy lit up a smoke, something he had picked up just recently to try and calm his nerves. He felt lost since parting with Ivy. She may have betrayed him, which really tore his heart to pieces, but she had been his little dark Ivy.

He missed her a lot and it was fraying his nerves badly. Sometimes he swore, just swore he heard her voice whispering his name in his ear from time to time. Made him jump the first time and nearly scream. He wondered if he might be unraveling somehow. Losing it, he couldn't do that now, he couldn't lose his touch, not now. Not when he was so close to the ultimate piece de resistance in his artwork. Not now. Just not now.

Troy eyed the trunk as the woman started screaming herself horse again, slamming her tied up fists on the underside of it. Not begging anymore at least. Hopefully she'd scream herself silent soon. He was waiting for her to do just that before popping the trunk open. He didn't want a repeat of the last bitch who tried to escape. The woman started to fall quiet just as Troy flicked his butt across the pathway into a small little ditch with stagnant water.

His gaze flicked around as he surveyed the area, making sure there were no prying eyes to catch him working. He'd become paranoid lately. Felt watched and couldn't shake a sense of doom and gloom. Troy had chalked that up to the grief of losing his Ivy, he figured it might settle soon enough though.

He hoped at least. He wasn't used to these feelings. Still, he also had this other problem. That agent. Leo was it. What was it about him that pulled on Troy, called to him even. Something different about this agent. He couldn't place his thumb on it. It bothered him that he couldn't quite figure it out.

THUMP. THUMP. THUMP

"Oh, for fucks sake woman, give it up, the inevitable is coming straight for you like a fucking freight train, accept it bitch." Troy growled at the trunk; a whimper floated back up at him in response that made him grin like a mad man.

"Sandy Sandra, met her at the beach. Hair as blonde as boxed bleach..." Troy began as he pulled out his keys, "Thought she was safe and sound, boy did that make her look like a silly clown."

Troy jammed the key into the trunk lock, and it swung up. Looking back at him were a pair of brown eyes. Her mouth had been taped over, but she had managed to pull it down, scratching her cheeks in the process. He clucked his tongue at her and shook his head while running his hand through her bleached blonde hair.

Her lip trembled and Troy smiled again, yes that's right sweet doe, you realize now what's going to happen don't you. He reached into the trunk and hooked his arm under her upper back and his other arm beneath her legs at the knees. She tried to dead weight him and Troy howled with laughter at her. Wasn't going to be that easy sweetie!

He winked at her which made her start to cry uncontrollably again. That only served to make him laugh harder. Good god, the women he had picked lately were pussies. Where'd the fighters go? Troy started toward the metal door hidden away in his forest. The closer he got the more unnerved he became. Ever since Ivy he'd been more and more uneasy about his workspace.

It felt like she was haunting it and him. He had even had to move her jar to a lower, out of the way shelf because those eyes, floating, staring, always staring and judging. He unlocked the metal door and the hum of the overheads blared to life. The one light at the end of the hallway flickered and died out with a pop that made both his doe and him jump.

Fuck me. She was staring at him, wide-eyed. Searching his face for any signs of humanity he supposed, none here boo, Troy mused to himself. He started down the hallway, his shoes clicking along the concrete floor loudly. At the end, where the light bulb had popped into its own version of death, shadows were dancing in the darkness. A streak of movement made Troy pause, unsure of how to react. Am I coming undone he wondered. He swore he saw green eyes staring back at him low to the ground.

Sandy Sandra wriggled in his arms, forcing Troy to put her to standing on her bare feet in the hallway. She took a few steps backward into the darkness causing Troy to back up and stare past her with a frown. Were the green eyes moving, no can't be. It's just a trick of the shadows, there's nothing there. It's nothing. Pull your shit together Troy, '*the doll!*' That last one felt like someone had screamed it inside his head and Troy flinched then lunged at Sandy Sandra as she tried to flee past him in the hallway.

Troy spun on his heels and realized he hadn't closed and locked the bunker door. Bitch was making a break for it and his stupid ass gave her the opportunity. He lashed out and kicked her ankle, ripping her feet out from under her. The thud of her landing on the concrete floor was loud and the grunt that came out of her told Troy she was fully winded.

Good, stupid bitch. Troy started laughing uncontrollably, it was a mix of seething rage and lunacy. Not a good mix for Sandy Sandra as the shick of the blade was followed by her howling scream while Troy bore down between her shoulder blades still laughing maniacally.

He was mindful of where his blade ripped through her, he didn't want her to bleed out right away or die of a collapsed lung, he wanted her immobile but feeling. Nicking the spinal cord just enough for both to be accomplished. She would feel his work and she wouldn't be able to escape it. He would make her pay for trying to run from her destiny and him.

☙

It had been a short work of Sandy Sandra. She screamed through the whole thing. He was sure she would have passed out at some point, but he had to admit the bitch had been tough after all. Troy shook his head as he made another small cut to his doe, he was almost done with the alterations of her face. His creations started out like a broken doll, but it was Troy's job and calling to fix the broken dolls of the world by stitching them back together.

It was always the mouth that needed the most work from him because the dolls always talked too much didn't they. You stupid dumb ass, can't you get it right. What did I ever do to you Troy. What's your problem Troy, did you pee yourself again stupid boy. Come here, don't you dare cry, you're a boy not a pussy. You're just like your mother. ***Sinner!***

Troy had hated that woman with a passion growing up. His aunt Gracie certainly hadn't lived up to her namesake. The old hag had been a nasty, mean old woman. She would spank him with a switch she'd make him go pick from her trees in her back garden or she'd burn him on his arms with her cigarillos. She'd find small petty things to spank him for or make him sit on his bare knees in the corner on uncooked rice grains for hours on end staring up at the Jesus cross she had on the wall.

Pray for your damned soul Troy, pray that you don't end up like your mother. 'In hell fire for your sins just like her' she would tell him. You see, his mother had died, committed suicide. Slit her own mouth wide open then opened her own throat after removing her own eyes from their sockets.

She had done so right in front of him at the tender age of eight. That's why he had been sent to aunt Gracie to live with, there had been no one else to take him.

His mother had been a single mother. She had also been a schizophrenic. His aunt, her sister from another father, had cruelly told him that his mother probably heard the voices tell her to do it like the bat shit crazy bitch that she was. His aunt Gracie had screamed horrifically as he had carved her up. He fucked it up though, "blew his load" a little too quickly and he was sloppy about it. That art piece he had to break apart and discard in creative ways. His first attempt at art with a broken doll had been an utter failure.

Then again, at the tender age of eighteen he supposed he was still learning the grace it took to be an artist of this caliber. I mean, every artist had to start at the bottom right.

Troy sighed softly as he picked up the needle to stitch the doe together. His hands knew their work well enough. Dip and stitch, dip and stitch. The rhythmic movements calming Troy's frayed and tattered nerves. It had taken him a long time to perfect this dip and stitch movement. Shattering a lot of dolls to do it and hunting a lot of doe too. Dolls? Where did that come from, why was he calling them dolls now? When did he start calling them dolls? Troy frowned, his hand pausing mid stitch, trying to figure out where he had heard that term, why he would even start calling his doe a doll. It was unsettling.

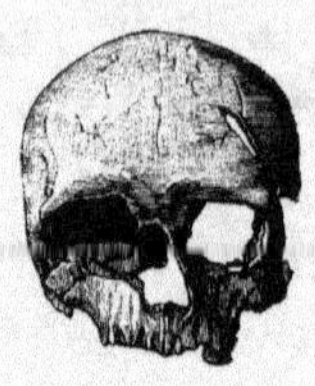

THE KILLERS WENT IN TWO BY TWO, HOORAH, HOORAH!

Leo was sitting on the couch, staring at a picture of the unidentified victim from earlier today. Her empty sockets called him to see their truth. Pools of darkness in the photo. He could almost make out her eyes where they should have been. Why the piece of paper, why? Leo rolled the question around in his head, grasping at it, letting it go, rolling it around again.

"My part to play in..." He tossed the photo on the coffee table in frustration and scooped up his pad Thai take out, angrily stabbing at the food with his chopsticks.

Why? 'Part to play', he lovingly took care of this victim, loved her, possibly they loved her, there were two killers now. Leo jerked forward, sitting up straight and stared at the photo on the table harder. Something, two. Two killers, my part to play in - ***it***.

His brow raised, the chop sticks poised, balancing delicately on his fingers, teetering. "*Son of a bitch*," Leo yelped stiffly, "She isn't his victim, she's his accomplice! She's the second killer!"

"What was that Leo?" A disembodied voice called out from the bathroom.

"The current victim, she's the second killer." Leo called back, "That's why the change in M.O."

Ari stepped out of the bathroom to regard Leo for a moment. He was sitting on the couch with just a towel wrapped around his waist, eating the left-over pad Thai from last night. Ari thought that was kind of gross eating leftovers that had been out overnight, but the man had weird habits sometimes. She wondered if he ever got sick from those bad habits. Smiling, she walked over to him and straddled his lap, pulling the pad Thai out of his hand.

"You know that isn't a healthy habit right?" Ari whispered playfully at him and put the leftovers on the table.

Leo leaned back against the couch and eyed Ari. The soft slope of the top of her breasts peeking out of her partly buttoned up shirt. How distracting. He smiled softly, seemed they had great sex, but they never could get along in a relationship. She has great tits Leo thought as he leaned toward her. He kept eye contact with her as she moved in to kiss him on the mouth, he felt himself stir hungrily in the core of his being. His heartbeat thudding against his throat. They may not have a great relationship but gods this woman knew how to make his heart skip beats.

☙

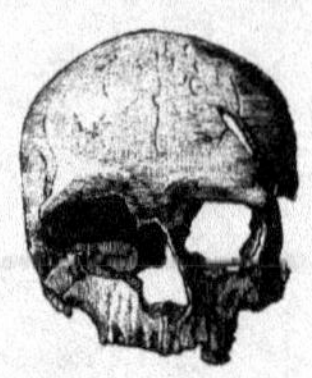

THE DEVIL BESIDE HER

Troy side eyed the woman while pretending to look down at a chart. The city morgue smelled like he remembered it. Disinfectant and latex with formaldehyde and rubbing alcohol. He was wearing a lab coat and pretending to look busy. Ari was bustling around the DB like a little busy bee. Making notes and taking samples. It was Ivy she was working on. Swabbing the empty eye sockets, cheeks and taking skin scrapings and fingernail samples.

Ivy's chest was spread wide open, organs missing and in their sample containers. Her stomach contents were on the side table, Her last meal with Troy slowly rotting away in her stomach acids along with his poison ivy concoction he'd fed her. Brain, heart, liver, kidneys. All of them weighed, sampled from and tagged and charted. Troy had to admit, Ari was pretty thorough about her work, he could appreciate that.

"The subject has had her eyes removed, with the ocular nerves missing completely. They were not found at the body dump site. According to reports and evidence a folded piece of lined paper was found in the left eye socket."

"It was the right eye socket Ari."

Troy smirked as Ari jumped ten feet out of her skin when he spoke suddenly. It amused him greatly, gave him a thrill really. Ari was staring at him hard, it made Troy twitch a little bit. She couldn't possibly recognize him from school could she? Troy froze for a moment when Ari came to the realization that she did indeed recognize him.

"You're that guy who dropped out of med school aren't you?"

"Yes I am, hello Ari. Nice to see you again."

"What are you doing here?"

"I am the wolf in your grandmother's clothing Ari, don't you know?"

"What?! What are you rambling on about?"

"All the better to carve you up with my pretty," Troy whispered menacingly at Ari, grabbing at her sharply and yanking her close.

Ari tried to scream, she really did try but it was too late. Troy had her and was covering her mouth with a rag soaked in something. Ari's eyes widened when she figured out what that something was on the rag, chloroform! She had time enough to think the word chloroform and shit in succession before blacking out and knocking her side table over, spilling all her coroner tools all over the place.

She drifted into the darkness with Troy's maniacal giggling in her ears while he whispered how she, his new doll, would be used to lure a certain someone out into his play ground, that the huntsman would become the hunted. Ari whimpered as the darkness finally took hold and Troy picked her up, placed her in a body bag on the table next to him. He zipped the body bag up while a grin spread across his face. Time to go sweet little dollie. Time to play a game, let's have some fun shall we! Troy pulled a card from his pocket. On it was a little note to his newly minted and favorite agent of the year.

Agent Desbrates, or may I call you Leo? I have something that belongs to you Leo. You might want to hurry and come find us before the game begins and the doe becomes the doll.

Below his message was the map to the bunker in his forest. Well, not quite but close to the bunker in his forest. It was a map to a clearing close enough to the bunker that Troy could subdue his prey in and then bring it home. He had a bone to pick with Leo and now was the time to pick it. Troy aimed to pick it clean too.

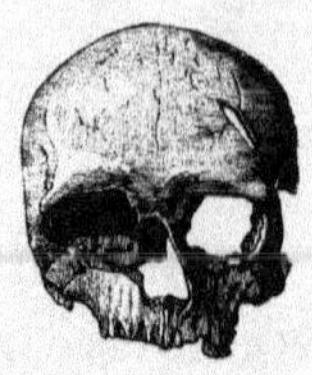

DEVILS ADVOCATE

Leo frowned as he put his cell phone back down on the desk. Why wasn't Ari answering his texts. She wasn't picking up his calls either. He knew she was working on the latest Jane Doe, the one they'd found in the park and Leo had figured out was the second killer. Shuffling papers and staring blankly at his computer screen Leo sighed softly, Leo was guessing he was in the doghouse now. For whatever it was he'd supposedly done. He was sure he'd find out sooner or later what annoying habit of his had pissed Ari off this time. That woman was a finicky creature. Leo leaned back in his chair, pulling the evidence bag with the lined paper piece out of the Doll Face Case folder. He stared at it for a moment. The faded curved lines of handwriting.

Why was it familiar? His eyes roamed around the room and landed on his lecture notes sitting on the filing cabinet. When it hit him he grunted as if he'd been sucker punched in the face, hard. Of course, that Ivy lady from the Ripper class. Leo got up and dumped the notes on the floor, sifting through them. He was looking for something. Aggravated, he tossed the case files for his lecture over his shoulder and they landed with a comical flurry of papers across the carpet. Scattered papers like scattered victims. A few slipping under another filing cabinet along his office wall and another few floating as if pulled by strings under his desk. ***There!*** There it was, the note that the woman had handed him that day at the lecture hall. The woman who had left him feeling oddly discombobulated and drifting.

'LENORE'

That's all the note had said, in that same curved, scripted lines of handwriting. The same loops in the "O" and "L" as the faded piece of paper that had come from the other killer's right eye socket.

"Ivy. It's you isn't it Ivy?"

A thump behind Leo startled him and he had to catch himself from falling on his ass from a crouched position. He turned around expecting someone, maybe, Agent Bast to be standing there tapping a foot and sneering at him; but, there was no one there.

"Odd." Leo shivered, did it just get cold in here he started to wonder to himself as he stood up, catching the corner of his desk on the back of the shoulder, "Gods damn it. Seriously!"

Leo stood fully with the note in his hand from his lecture bag. His back to his desk, studying the script like handwriting when it happened again. THUMP, but this time it was a thump and slide sound. Leo sucked in air through pursed lips and swung around to stare whatever or whoever was there in the face only to be met, with nothing. Leo looked down at his boots and his brow raised.

A book, there was a letter and tucked in that was a photo. It was upside down, the photo, but that Bic pink pen ink on the back was familiar. Just as familiar as the note in his hand with Lenore on it. Leo scooped up the photo, first looking at the back of it. In a kid-like version of the script like handwriting on the note in his other hand that matched the writing on the piece of paper from Ivy's right eye socket, were three names and the year the photo was taken. Leo went white and flipped the photo over to look at it. It was her! It was HIM! Leo's jaw unhinged then firmly clamped into a tight gnashing of teeth. Troy. How long had it been? This photo, that summer. Leo exhaled slowly, what a gut punch he'd just taken. He looked at the book on the floor and picked it and the letter up now.

He slowly flipped through the book, yeah it was hers alright, then he turned his attention to the letter. That script like handwriting again, this time adult like, aged like a soft, perfect chardonnay. How could he have not recognized those beautiful green eyes from his childhood at his lecture that day. Her eyes, how did he not see her. He'd been in love with her as a kid but back then that kind of love didn't sit well with the adults or society. He didn't sit well for what he was back then with the adults or society.

He'd kept it to himself, loved her from afar besides it seemed Troy and her had a thing when they were kids and he hadn't wanted to step between them and what they had. Family didn't do that to family and the Loser's Club had been their tiny little misfit family. He couldn't remember when they'd lost contact with each other. That summer had been difficult to say the least. There were secrets from that summer that would have made his supervisor bare her teeth at him in a way that would make her screaming at him more palpable. That summer had made the Summer of Sam look like a cruise party compared to it. At least, for them as kids it felt like that. Leo opened up the letter, it was addressed directly to him. Her scripted, soft handwritten loop-de-loops across the page.

Len .. Leo: Please find in this book, my diary, the evidence you need for your Doll Face case and your Asylum case. I'm sorry that the asylum case hurt you so deeply, that was my fault. It was nice to see you again Leo. How I've missed you so much! Your eyes will always tell me who you are, even if others don't know the real you.

Lovingly, Ivy

Leo smiled, a few tears running down his cheeks. He wished he had just noticed sooner, had seen her sooner. Could he have saved her from Troy? There'd always been an oddness about Troy, even when they were growing up especially after his Auntie had left him alone that one spring.

Leo had hated his Aunt Gracie. Mean old coot that she'd been always ranting about sin, brimstone and hellfire. That spring Troy had acted funny, always with that backpack he was carting around for the first few weeks of spring. Always preoccupied, talking to himself and muttering quietly. He'd come out with them all around town with a heavy backpack and always seemed to come home a little lighter in that backpack. Leo had always suspected Aunt Gracie hadn't just disappeared on an extended visit to family like Troy claimed she did. Leo was about to flip the diary back open when his office door swung open hard, banging the handle into the wall and taking out a chunk of plaster. It was Agent Smith.

"Boss man, it's Ari. She's gone missing." Agent Smith gasped as he tried to catch his breath.

"What do you mean she's missing?"

"The boys down at the city morgue said she disappeared and hasn't been back. They thought maybe she'd taken a lunch break but Ari never leaves her DBs unfinished. She always finishes first before hand. Then they found this."

Agent Smith produces a note card in an evidence bag between them, Leo snatched it out of Smith's hand and stared at it hard. Son of a bitch. It was a note from, of all people, Troy. Telling Leo where to find him and Ari. It seems Troy had snatch and grabbed Ari and wanted Leo to pursue.

"You know it's a trap right Agent Desbrates?"

"Yeah, it's a trap but what other choice do I have? Give me five and we roll out."

As Leo shooed Agent Smith out of his office, slamming the door, he caught sight of something that made him pale and clamp a hand over his mouth to keep from screaming involuntarily. In the dust on his desk was scrawled in the same script like handwriting as Ivy's the words, Loser's Club. Leo looked up with tears brimming from his eyes, he rolled his head from side to side and forced himself to breathe slower as he tried to calm himself down. He smiled weakly and nodded after a few moments whispering to himself as he rushed out the door of his office.

"Thank you Ivy. Thank you."

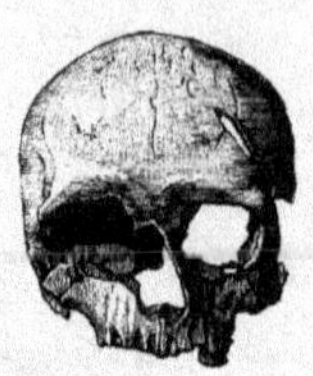

THE AGENT MAN WHO WORE JIMMY CHOO SHOES

Agent Smith was grasping wildly at the holy shit handle and hollering at Leo to slow down in the bush trails, grimacing and twitching at every sharp corner Leo took with his Dodge Charger Hellcat. Screaming around bends and skidding through left and right turns as he stared at the map to see the next turn to take. Smith was looking pale and green at the same time when Leo cursed loudly as he nearly crashed into three birch trees at a fork in the dirt road.

He had to stop, back up and make the turn at the birch trees that the map told him to. He didn't notice the door when they went past it. It was too dark to notice at night unless you knew it was there. Even at that, it wasn't where the map was telling Leo to go anyway. He grunted a few more fucks into the night sky as he rounded another corner, praying to whatever god or gods might be listening that Ari was still alive, that he could still save her. He couldn't help save the other her when they were kids. That had weighed heavily in his mind for all of his adult life.

He had been helpless to save her or her sister, Ivy. They'd only been kids. He remembered that day too well. He still had nightmares about it to this day. He was sure it was what caused some of his "bad habit" neurotic tendencies. It was also what drove Leo to be an FBI agent in the first place. Troy, Leo and her. They'd grown up together in some trying times. All of them from broken homes. Him, the dumpster kid as his nickname was then, with a foster family. Troy with his Aunt Gracie and her with her sister and parents.

He was ignored for the most part, a paycheck to the foster family he was with. He hadn't had any family left, abandoned, left behind, alone. That was the idea behind the nickname he'd been given by the playground kids, one that had stuck with him for a very long time, dumpster kid, the forgotten, the abandoned ones. Troy, he'd heard through playground gossip and snippets here and there from Troy himself, had been sent to his Auntie because his mother had committed suicide in front of him. Her, she was the one who had it the worst of them though. She had her own flesh and blood become the monster in her of her childhood nightmares.

Which in turn ended her childhood prematurely. Leo remembered the day it happened, the day her childhood got ripped so thoroughly from her and then murdered and buried. She'd come to them sobbing and shaking. Barely able to get the rotting words of what had happened out of her mouth. Troy and Leo had looked at each other and nodded, knowing full well what needed to be done. She'd already wrapped her sister in the blanket with her teddy bear. Troy and he had taken her sister and wrapped her into the living room rug too so they could easily move the body into the bushes behind their row houses on the street.

They'd taken turns carrying her sister over one shoulder until they found the spot that would hide their dreadful secret from the world forever. They'd even taken turns shoveling, her too. Once they had dug far enough they placed the body in the deep grave. Troy had said it had to be at least six feet so that animals and the elements wouldn't dig her back up. Where a kid finds that kind of information had been beyond Leo at the time. She'd stood there, swaying and sobbing for a while staring into the final resting place they had made for her sister. Leo had tried to put his arm around her but Troy had shoved himself between them, throwing his arm around her instead and pulling her away from the grave.

The teddy bear's ears, nose and eyes were poking out from under the blanket and rug, staring sullenly back at him. It made Leo shiver even now as an adult. They did it out of love for her, taking her secret and burying it in the ground and carrying it for her. They were strong enough to bear it, she hadn't been then and Leo wasn't sure she had ever been strong enough in the living. He hoped that she was now in her passing.

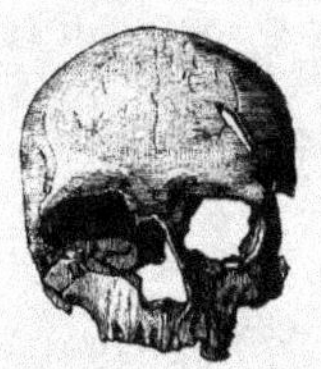

THE DEVIL YOU KNOW

"Stop Agent Desbrates, stop."

Leo grunted as he slammed on the brakes and threw the Hellcat in park at the same time causing the car to lurch unnaturally. Leo was about to turn toward Agent Smith when something caught his eye at the last second. The sound of shattering glass, the thump and then grunt from Agent Smith and then seeing the slow blossom of red spreading on Smith's shirt caught Leo off guard for a split second. He had time enough to think he got lucky as he swung the driver's side door open and rolled out of the car when the second shot hit Agent Smith's head dead center sending blood, brains and bone all over the inside of Leo's car.

"Well that's a mess ain't it Agent?"

Leo growled as he pulled himself around the ass end of his car, hugging the metal with his back. He slid around the other side, peering over the trunk quickly to try and get a bead on where Troy was. He didn't see Troy but he did see Ari. He bore his teeth, wincing at the sight of her chained in the middle of the clearing. It seems Troy had driven a metal spike into the ground as far as it would go and attached a chain to it. He'd chained Ari by the throat with a metal ring and padlock.

Ari stared at him, pleading with him for help with her eyes. She was gagged but her hands and feet were unbound and free. It was a start at least.

"She's a pretty little dollie isn't she?" Troy laughed while rattling Ari's chain, "bit of a fighter too. What exciting times Agent Desbrates, Leo."

"What do you want Troy?"

It knocked him off center completely to hear his name, Leo could see that it did. He smiled as Troy stood there, swaying a little with eyes wide and mouth agape.

Leo moved quietly up the body of his car, still hugging close to it, listening intently for any movements that might indicate Troy was launching a physical attack.

"What's wrong Troy, one of your dollies caught your tongue?"

"Fuck you Leo! What do you know about my dolls," Troy shook his head violently, slapping it with the heel of his hand and muttered get out, get out of my head bitch! "***Doe***, what do you know about my precious doe?"

Leo hunkered down, bowing his head, thinking. It seems he's lost his mind, he's spiraling, losing it. I can use this to my advantage. Peeking around the headlight of the Hellcat Leo nodded at Ari, mouthing words at her trying to convey to her not to move, to stay put and he was coming for her. After a few moments it looked like Ari seemed to understand and laid down in the grass trying to make herself as small as she possibly could. Leo leaned back against the car and shouted out at Troy,

"What happened Troy, did Ivy piss you off?"

"She didn't appreciate my work Leo, I thought she was the one, I thought she would be the one but no, she wasn't was she?"

"So, you turned her into one of your dolls, took your trophies from her. Treated her like she was nothing. Like a dirty little secret? Is that it Troy, is that what happened? She didn't do what you wanted her to and you punished her for it didn't you, just like Aunt Gracie right?"

There was silence from Troy, it was a deafening silence, a dangerous silence. It was like a dog lip licking before the bite. That strange silence before the storm hits where the light of day goes all wonky and funny looking. Leo would have preferred anything but the racing thud of his heart in his chest and the sounds of his car indicator dinging away into the dark of the night and that calm before the storm silence.

"Who the fuck are you? How? How do you know about her? Who are you Leo, I demand you tell me. Shut Up! I am trying to think straight, get out of my head, get out of my head little Ivy flower. Get out!"

"Losing it much Troy? What's wrong, Ivy got you all twisted around does she? Can't bury her six feet at least can you? Is the teddy bear haunting your dreams yet Troy? Or has it always haunted your dreams? Can you see it's black, dark eyes staring back at you from its shallow dirt grave?"

CS

Troy froze, staring at the car in front of him, jaw unhinged. There was no way Agent Desbrates could have ever known about that. That was a secret him and his Loser's Club had vowed to take to their graves. There wasn't any way this agent could know that unless he had been there or talked to one of the three of them. Think Troy my love, who is Leo? Who is he to you? Who am I, Ivy to you?

Shut up! I'm thinking. I'm losing my mind aren't I?

Yes, yes you are Troy, you are losing your ever loving mind.

Troy grunted as he caught movement at the front of the car, he swung his hand up and popped off a round at the car causing Agent Desbrates to pull back around the other side again.

"Behave Agent or I kill your pretty little girlie friend here."

Troy hated the gun but it was a necessity at the moment, he preferred his knives, touching them, being close to them. The dollies squeal more if you get closer. See, look the new dollie is trying to keep from screaming right now.

Look Troy! Troy looked down at the woman at his feet, she was hugging dirt, trying to stay quiet and still. He crouched beside her and grinned at her when tears started to roll down her cheeks. He could imagine how maniacal he might look to her. Her. Troy looked from Ari to the car and back again. Her. Leo. Smaller than the rest, shorter, built but small frame. Her. Leo. Lenore!

That's it Troy, there you go, you've got it now!

"Shut the fuck up and get out of my fucking head Ivy!" Troy screamed suddenly, startling Ari.

"Lenore. You sneaky bitch you. It's been a very long time hasn't it Dumpster Kid. Too long."

"Yes it has been but not long enough to be honest with you Troy." Leo looked around the front of the car, seeing Ari staring wide eyed and terrified back at him. He raised a brow when Ari started shaking her head but it was too late. Troy had circled around the car and Leo had missed it completely. Leo turned in time to catch the blade through the palm of his hand, the tip only a few millimeters away from his face.

"I'm going to make you my ultimate doll Leo. A masterpiece like no other. The hermaphrodite of dollies." Troy growled.

It was no use, Leo was pinned to the car by the sheer weight of Troy leaning into him. Leo struggled to gain footing but his boots were slipping in the dew covered grass. Ari was trying to scream with her gag but all it did was come out desperately muffled while Troy yanked the blade back roughly with a spray of blood slapping across his own face. He grinned and licked some of it off his lips. With a coppery metallic taste coating his throat Troy began to laugh hysterically. Pay attention Troy, you little sinner! The voice of his dead Aunt startled him back for a moment.

That was all his prey needed though wasn't it, a moment. Troy cursed as Leo slipped out from under him and rolled away to the front of the car where the headlights lit up part of the clearing. Troy lunged at Leo with the blade above his head. Stupid little boy, look at you now. Can't do anything right can you? Troy had a split second to tell his Aunt Gracie to kiss his ass before the shot Leo had taken hit its mark dead center mass on Troy. He kept going though, Troy couldn't feel a damn thing in his all encompassing rage. Troy, it's over, stop now. It was his little Ivy flower talking now. A few more shots from Leo and Troy was sinking to his knees in the grass in front of the car. Looking up into Leo's face Troy smirked.

"Wasn't easy growing up, was it Dumpster Kid?"

"No, no it wasn't Troy. We got the short end of the stick but she got it worse didn't she."

"You never told either, did you, not ever?"

"No Troy, No I didn't. We made a vow that day, a pact between the three of us."

"I wonder if my little dark Ivy flower is waiting for me?"

Troy laid down in the grass trying to catch his breath but they were only coming in snippets and wheezes here and there. He could feel darkness starting to creep over him. His vision was blurring now. Troy's brows furrowed, there were a second pair of feet next to Lenore's.

His name is Leo Troy not Lenore.

Is that you my sweet little Ivy flower?

Yes Troy, time to go. Come on.

"Janelle." Troy gasped.

"Yes Troy, Janelle." Leo answered.

Troy grunted his last few breaths out as Leo knelled beside him. Troy strained to look up at him with his last bit of energy. Instead of Leo's face he saw a photo. He knew what was written on the back in Bic pink ink when he saw the photo and smiled. That was a photo of a better time for them, one of the few good moments they'd all had where nothing mattered and the monsters couldn't touch you because you had each other.

Troy's last final moments passed quietly with a photo beside him of his childhood friends and an old friend from that photo knelled in the grass with him holding his hand as he bled out. In death Troy had finally escaped his childhood monster, his Aunt Gracie.

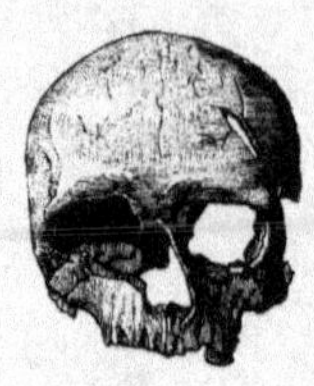

THE DEAD DONT STAY THAT WAY

Somehow, it seems like wandering around the vacuous dank and somewhat blah afterlife that I would be able to reflect on my life. There is not much else to do here. I wish I could tell you that death leads to some wondrous world in which a group of angels descend in white robes and you get to see the face of God. No, there is no god here. There is no devil here. There is nothing here, other than the darkened shades of your past, reflecting in mirrors around you.

Sitting here seeing the faces of those I killed haunt me, just as I, undoubtedly am haunting you. In one of the mirrors, the one that holds the furthest memories of my mind, the mirror that is the most scared from its ties into the worlds beyond, its sheen somewhat patinae, somewhat less mirror and more just glass. The difference is not apparent to the untrained eye, but it's there. As if glass holds a 'ghost' of a thing, and a mirror holds that ghost like a prisoner. A mirror tells you the truth, glass does not. Glass lies to you, glass shows you only what you want to see.

Glass displays the gaudy fashions draped on mannequins like loose flesh. Glass displays the pretty cakes that now I crave to taste one more time, glass encourages the eyes to feed on what they see beyond. We become unnatural voyeurs in a concrete prison for which we seek escape. The mirror however, the sly whore, is the dead eye thing that shows every scar, every wound, every hit, slap, punch, stab. Its truth cannot be hidden, you look at the reflection there and see only the raw natural truth of yourself.

That is what is around me now. It is the truth, raw, unyielding and I am captured by it. They laugh at me, keep flicking on and off the truth that is unrepentant. What else did I expect? Those who evil wrought must then pay for the evil right? I feel the dark and damp around me, I hold my rotting flesh. I see the skin revealing bone, and the 'me' wasting away to be the faded thing in the dark. There is something there near me, I reach out, it's an almost faded book! No, not a book, a diary, it's mine! I see it, I know it. It seems so surreal to me as I turn it again and again in my hands. I recall it, and there in the first page is the day I met the dumpster kid.

Yes Lenore, I knew, I knew who you were Leo. Why you didn't see me that day in your lecture room, I don't know, but I knew you. Your eyes have the same gleam as they once did when we were kids. I feel you near me and the mirrors flash. I see your desk, and you're standing there with my note! The only thing I'd written on it was Lenore that day. I barely can hold my own weight as I struggle to stand, I know it's time, it's time to show you, to tell you, to reach out to the present, to affect what sits there on your desk right now.

Shuffling over to the mirror, I take my hand and push it through the glass, and flick the book that's on your desk, just a push - just one - THUMP. I am using any energy I have, just a nudge, just a nudge. I see the book, it finally falls. He knows now, he knows. The paper falls out, the letter written in my hand, but the photo, it's the photo I want him to see. He knows the names scrawled on the back in cheap Bic pink ink, there we are now Leo, look. Yes! Yes, see it now. I see him unfold the note, he knows, he sees and I pull my hand back, I only have a small amount in me left.

My hand now blackened from reaching through the mirror, you are almost all gone now Ivy the wind whispers, his mirror chimes, I know. I know. There in the diary, the one that I left for that FBI agent and now that I am dead, I know it all. I understand now. I reach out with the other hand this time, etching into the dust on his desk. Come on Ivy, focus, the words appear as if from nowhere, the words on his desk etched there in time - LOSER'S CLUB - he whispers Thank you Ivy, Thank You.

Before he says another word, I fall back and land on the hard wooden floors, there is nothing here, it is cold, empty, soulless. There are the lamenting of the others, the mirrors, the glass, the clock, the ticking, my heart long silenced, my mouth tied and stitched closed, I am voiceless like the a doe, like his other dolls. There the past at last is in my reach. The mirror reflects back to the house, to the room, there is dad. The bodies, the bodies, my hands and something isn't right. I am with the losers again but something else, something claws its way inside.

I see a field, and in that field a tree, a tree that's roots go deep into the ground. We stand there with shovels, yes there is a 'we'. I recall my favorite poem: "You cannot have a funeral for your mother, without also having a funeral for yourself" but instead the word mother swirls in my head adding another to it. It is true one cannot bury the things it loves. Love is more powerful than hate, than wounds but it doesn't always prevent the monsters from sneaking in. There in the place of our youth, there lies a grave, under a tree. It has no name, and yet it does. They helped me then, their little broken doll.

You see, we all knew each other, once, long ago. They knew the dead eyed doll, because they took me from the monsters in my bedroom. They, having monsters of their own, kept me from remembering, they helped me forget but now I see it. There in that grave, the grave with no name, holds my last secret. I see the last night in the house, and the words of the poem are stricken with red drips of a heart that beats no more, the word mother is replaced with sister. You see, one night we were hiding, and she made a noise, and I squeezed. I squeezed to protect us, to protect her and there in my arms she was lifeless. Her treasured toy teddy bear dangled from her arm and her dead eyes like the dolls all around my room, like her teddy bear's black beaded eyes.

I couldn't move because that time dad had a weapon, and the weapon had our names cut deep in its grooves. It was hunting us, he was hunting us and he was going to kill us that night. It was two days later, that I moved from that closet with her, the smell, the flies, her dead lifeless body. Her eyes saying you killed me, you took my life. I wrapped her in a blanket, I kissed her head, I wept for her, I hated myself, I hated the teddy bear, and I hated this life. In that moment, there was no choice, I took whatever was human and ripped it from me, she would be my escape.

I snuck out and fled to the losers, I told them, they said nothing because those who live with monsters sometimes learn when not to speak, this was a secret we would keep, and bury, and wipe away but as I told you, things don't ever stay buried especially when they are wrong things, unspoken things, broken things that need mending. The losers came back to the house, we snuck in and took her out, we buried her there, teddy and all. I went back to my house that day, I picked up my stuff, I took the drugs that Dumpster Kid, Lenore gave me, the drugs to forget, the pills to not remember and there, in that grave, lies Ivy.

Yes, I am not Ivy, I never was. She was buried there, buried deep, her lifeless little body still looking up at me. What is my name you ask? What is the name that now is uttered in the voice of an FBI agent, that same agent that was the Dumpster Kid? That agent that is now known as Leo. What is the name that Troy heard, that he recalled and was my undoing. It was so stupid for this broken doll to have that diary with that name written in a thoughtful place, a place that I thought was only seen by me.

I hear now her voice, a hand reaches, sissy it's me, I am here, come find me and a giggle that sends shivers through me to my bones. I see it all so clearly, call me Ivy no more - my name is Janelle, and I am the girl that killed her sister. The girl whose friends helped her bury her sister, her secret and her name in the dirt in the bushes behind their houses.

Time seems to have passed now. I am now free, the mirrors shatter around me, glass falling all over the floor. I stand, I feel my legs, I am somewhat whole again, maybe there is something else to this. I feel a pair of shoes behind me and I turn - it's him.

"Glad to see me, darling" he says, sweeping me in his arms. We dance like broken marionettes, limbs not quite right, not quite together even, like a true dance macabre. We are twisted and rotting and dancing together.

"Yes, my beloved, my Troy, my darling" I reply. The wind whisks through and picks up the glass that is shattered on the floor. It swirls around us like a tornado, there is no pain and he looks into my eyes, I see his fresh wounds, his blood, the smell of his flesh and I reach my hand down to my side, I fold into him.

"Forgive me, my beloved?" He asks tentatively.
I reach down and there, the knife, there is the blade. I pick it up, I plunge it in his fresh wound.
"Never!" I say, and it's done now.

The light pours in and blinds me at first and then there I am in the meadow, in the place where there is a tree, where a grave once stood. The grave gone now, and in its place is a group of honeysuckles waving in the wind. I look out and hear her voice, "Come on Janelle, let's go play hopscotch."

"Coming, Ivy, coming." I reply

Maybe, just maybe there is a heaven after all......

"Grief will never truly be done with you" -Amanda Lovelace

EPILOGUE

WHEN THE MONSTERS LOSE

The aftermath of the Doll Face case investigation had been brutal but not as brutal as the Asylum case one had been. Leo had managed, for the second time in his career to avoid being canned completely from the FBI. He didn't do field work anymore on account of his wife Ari asking him to take a "desk job". That and his hand ached much of the time now. The old wound from Troy ached the most when the wind howled just before the rain would fall.

He was a professor instead at Quantico teaching young budding profilers how to profile serial killers, mercy killers and family annihilators. He still taught his Ripper class as well. It was pretty popular these days. He still got the collective gasp every time he made the suggestion that Jack's other victims were substitutes for his real intended victim. The Doll Face case had become a bit of an infamous case for him. With the help of Janelle's diary he was able to close three cases in fact.

The Asylum case that had left his career with a black mark in his personnel files, the Doll Face case and an unknown to authorities case from his childhood. The courts had deemed the Ivy case an accidental death. While Janelle, Troy and himself, then Lenore had hidden the death from the authorities it was deemed unintentional obstruction of justice and that children of that age did not understand the magnitude nor the ramifications of what they had done. They were simply trying to survive an abusive environment while attempting to maintain their self preservation as individuals and a group.

They found Ivy's little body still buried beneath that tree in the bush behind those row houses, the teddy bear falling to ragged pieces when Leo had picked it up. They gave her a proper burial right next to her sister Janelle. It also came to light, even though they couldn't find her body and likely never would, that Troy had murdered his aunt in their shared family home, dismembered her body into pieces and disposed of those body parts all over the neighborhood over the course of a few weeks.

They came to the conclusion that this event was likely the trigger event for Troy and what was the driving force in his serial killings. He was repeating his first kill with subsequent victims trying to find the thrill he had with that first kill. It was also concluded that his victims were replacements for his already dead Aunt Gracie and the post humus mutilations for a symbol of his mother's trauma she had caused Troy by committing suicide in front of him at a very young age.

As for Janelle, then using her sister's name Ivy, they believed Troy had groomed her to be his accomplice being that he was the dominant personality taking charge over her submissive personality. They believed that Troy triggered in her the same instinct to kill while encouraging the behavior and prey drive that had been dormant. They noted that although Ivy had killed, she was not like Troy, it was not for her enjoyment, but to silence the trauma triggers. Each kill was a placeholder for the man that caused the death of her sister and abused Ivy as a child. Each body was an attempt to kill him, but instead it made her weaker in the dominant personality's eyes, in Troy's eyes and she, like the others, became his victim.

When Ivy, Janelle had finally stepped back from him and tried to go to the authorities Troy then turned his anger on her and made her one of his killing spree victims. If not for this event that triggered Troy's spiral into insanity Leo believed he would still be looking for his serial killer, that the Asylum case would never have been solved and their childhood secrets would have haunted him to this day.

"Are you coming to the dinner table daddy? Mommy says hurry up."

Leo looked up from his lecture notes and smiled at his daughter. Ari and Leo had to go the route of sperm donor considering Leo was a post op transgendered female to male. Ari was pregnant with their second, waiting for the pregnancy bubble to burst any day now too. He rubbed his hand, fingers tracing the scars there from Troy's blade.

"I'm coming my darling Ivy." Leo said as he scooped her up and tossed her in the air making her squeal and giggle delightfully.

When she was born, Leo made a vow to her, not his Ivy but the other Ivy and to Janelle too. That this Ivy would have a childhood free of monsters, free of pain and despair. That this Ivy would have the life that they should have had and deserved.

"Daddy?" Ivy cocked her head to one side as she peaked over his shoulder.

"Yes Ivy?" Leo said quizzically, "What is it sweetheart?"

Behind Leo was a shimmer of light in the mirror hanging on the wall in her daddy's study that had caught Ivy's eye. In that mirror were two little girls smiling back at her. They faded before Ivy could ask who they were and she simply shrugged her shoulders and smiled in her daddy's face.

"Nothing but I love you daddy!" Ivy squealed happily.

"I love you to the moon and back baby girl." Leo chuckled back while walking out the door with his daughter in his arms, "Hungry baby girl? Yeah, let's go eat, shouldn't keep mama waiting should we?"

BIOGRAPHY

Larisa Hunter is the President of The Three Little Sisters LLC. She is the mother of a beautiful daughter, and wife to a devoted husband. She lives in California where she runs a publishing house and home made craft business.

Born in Montreal, Quebec and now residing in Northern Ontario. A practicing eclectic, solitary Druidic Shaman. Graphics designer and author of the Indie published book THESE CHAINS. Owner and operator of Black Cat Editing. Deejay and co-owner of the local Elliot Lake,Ontario entertainment business Mobile Sounds. Daughter, Sister, Wife, Mother, Woman.

The Three Little Sisters

The Three Little Sisters is an indie publisher that puts authors first. We specalize in the strange and unusual. From titles about pagan and heathen spirituality to traditional fiction we bring books to life.

https://the3littlesisters.com

www.ingramcontent.com/pod-product-compliance
Lightning Source LLC
Chambersburg PA
CBHW070359200726
48294CB00003B/1003

* 9 7 8 1 9 5 9 3 5 0 2 8 6 *